COBWEB DREAMS

ROSIE CHAPEL

First printing 2019
ISBN: 978-0-6488365-0-6 (Paperback)
ISBN: 978-0-6485283-2-6 (e-book)

Ulfire Pty. Ltd.
P.O. Box 1481
South Perth
WA 6951
Australia

www.rosiechapel.com

Cover Designed by Lisa Miller with Got You Covered

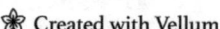 Created with Vellum

To my Mum and Dad,
who introduced me to the magic of Mull,
more years ago, than I care to remember.
This is for you, with all my love.

Author's Note

In this context, a lay-by is a pull in off the road, usually wide enough to park at least three or four vehicles, but often able to accommodate quite a number. Can be tarmac, but more often than not, and especially on Mull, they are simply areas of cleared ground which have become accepted parking spots.

Cobweb Dreams

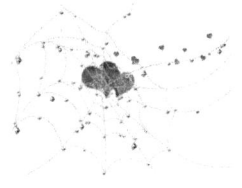

Rosie Chapel

1

MULL, SCOTLAND.

The dark shadow of Gribun Rocks towered in forbidding splendour ahead of her, while in complete contrast, Loch Na Keal, on her right, sparkled in the sunlight. Parking the car on a convenient grassy lay-by just off the roadside, Chloe Shepherd grabbed her hat and backpack then, making sure she locked the car, set out towards the cliffs.

Breathing in the heady scents floating on the air — bracken, the loamy earth, the slightly salty tang of the sea loch and just a hint of animal dung — to Chloe it was quintessentially Mull. She needed this, a whole month on her favourite Scottish isle. Aunt Meg, with whom she lived, had questioned Chloe's decision to use all of her annual holiday entitlement in such an isolated location.

Ten Days Earlier

"Won't you be lonely, dear?" Aunt Meg asked, perplexed at her niece's joyous expression upon receiving confirmation of her last-minute booking. A self-catering cottage in Salen, the little village not far from the Fishnish ferry terminal.

The pictures on the internet showed whitewashed walls, with dorma windows nestling in a grey, slate roof. The charmingly apportioned interior, while complete with all the modern fixtures and fittings, still retained a traditional cottage appearance.

"Lonely? Me? You know I am happiest on my own, Aunt Meg. I'll have my tablet, my laptop and my camera. I can't wait. I haven't been to Mull for about six years and I miss it." Chloe grinned at her aunt who was frowning. "Trust me, I will be fine. What could possibly happen?"

"Murder, mayhem, burglary, hoodlums, the list goes on. Honestly, Chloe, I think you are far too trusting. A young woman on her own would be an easy target."

"Goodness, aren't you the cheery soul? Way to be positive, not." Chloe chuckled, taking her aunt's hand and squeezing it gently. "I don't have anything anyone wants. I usually pass unnoticed, and I don't think I've upset anyone enough for them to contemplate murder." Ticking each one off on her fingers.

Meg Shepherd studied her niece. Quite tall, Chloe believed herself plain and uninteresting, mostly owing to the fact, she had been forced to listen to her parents moan about her lack of distinguishing characteristics most of her young life.

Thankfully, they were currently up to their armpits on a dig somewhere — Egypt she thought, or was it Morocco? Meg couldn't recall. They upped and offed on a regular basis, usually forgetting they had a daughter, in their rush to lose themselves in antiquity.

Archaeologists and professors, Chloe's mother and father were totally scatterbrained until it came to their favourite subject, and then they became astute, shrewd, brilliant, and sought after. Unfortunately, their daughter was not one of their favourite subjects, and they were wont to overlook her existence, often departing on expeditions without telling her, or anyone else.

When Meg discovered Chloe, at fourteen-years-old, had been left to fend for herself, while her esteemed parents vanished into the wilds of Syria, she put her foot down. Gathering up her niece, Meg informed Greg and Alison Shepherd, Chloe's home was now with her.

That was twelve years ago. Chloe, who saw her parents once in a blue moon, finished school, then applied and was accepted to do history at university. After graduation, unable to find work in her field, she landed a job as an administration clerk with a small company of motor insurance assessors.

She was a competent typist, had a friendly telephone manner, and her job did not entail dealing with the public too often. Chloe was innately reticent, preferring to remain in the background, never pushing herself forward, unless she had no alternative. Years of overhearing her parents informing anyone who would listen that she wouldn't amount to anything, ingrained in her psyche.

Meg's contemplation took in her niece's pale face, the result of long hours in an office and not enough fresh air. While Chloe believed she had no redeeming features, Meg begged to differ. Hair — the colour of ripened wheat, tumbled halfway down her back in shimmering waves although she mostly fashioned it into a plait or a sleek bun. Eyes — the most unusual grey, reminiscent of wet slate, currently a little shadowed.

When she smiled, which was rarely, her face lit up. Softly spoken, Chloe often surprised people when they discovered she owned a fiery temper and could shriek like a banshee when goaded, but it took a lot to rile her up. Her figure could only be described as curvy, but as Meg kept telling her, if she tried to follow the current fashion for skinny-minnies — with her considerable height — she would look gaunt.

Despite being uncomfortable in large groups, Chloe's polite

manner and reserved personality made her a favourite with the elderly and infirm, so much so, she was persuaded to join a program of volunteers, who kept an eye on those living in the local retirement village. Pop in, have a cuppa, chat for a while and make sure all was as it should be, any concerns reported to the warden.

Chloe found it rewarding and visited her charges every weekend. This rather curtailed any chance of a social life, but she loved listening to their tales and was happier with them than frequenting the nightclubs.

Now she was going to bury herself on a Scottish island for a month. Meg would never admit how worried she was about Chloe. The girl was entirely too solitary. She had missed out on all the normal antics teenagers get up to and seemed to avoid similar activities at uni. Even her job precluded any chance of meeting people, except those working in car repair yards, whom she visited periodically as part of her routine.

Meg dragged her attention back to Chloe's excited chatter, managing to sound as enthusiastic as her niece about the things the latter wanted to do while on Mull.

Present Day

Unaware of her aunt's concerns, Chloe was loving her holiday.

She had arrived two days previously, breaking her journey at a friendly bed and breakfast in Ballachulish, on the shores of Loch Leven. After checking into the B&B, she drove the short distance to Fort William, where she planned to have dinner and a leg stretch — not necessarily in that order.

Setting off early the following morning, Chloe caught both the Corran ferry traversing Lock Linnhe and then the Lochaline ferry to Fishnish across the Sound of Mull, without much delay, getting to Salen with the afternoon ahead of her.

Chloe spent her first full day on the island, driving into Tobermory — Mull's main town. Pottering about the colourful centre, she bought postcards and took a few requisite photographs, before stocking up on the essentials of life. This included a bottle of single malt whisky, brewed right there in the town.

Satisfied with her purchases, she enjoyed lunch at one of the cafés overlooking the harbour and then drove back to Salen. Unpacking and tidying everything away, she spent a quiet afternoon, reading in the sheltered garden at the rear of the cottage. It was peaceful and warm and, while sipping a well-earned whisky, Chloe realised she was beginning to unwind.

Now, today, she was raring to go. On her last visit, Chloe had taken a long walk under Gribun Rocks, every other day. There was something special about this part of the island.

The view to her right, out over the water towards the small islands of Eorsa and Inch Kenneth, and beyond to Ulva and Little Colonsay, was spectacular in every weather. The majestic cliff in front of her, rose a thousand feet from the loch.

The single-lane road along the base coupled with warnings of sporadic rockfalls, often deterred visitors, keeping it more or less peaceful — except at the peak of the tourist season.

Chloe decided to walk as far as the ruined croft where — legend told — a massive boulder dislodged during a wild storm, rolled down the cliff and crushed the croft, killing the newly married couple inside.

The tale was macabre and the ruined cottage a poignant reminder of the loss, but it happened three hundred years ago and, while sad for the couple, Chloe had no personal connection to them or the story. To her, it was simply a good place for which to aim.

She struck out, stopping now and again to take a photo, or to admire the changing views. An occasional car whizzed past, usually too fast for the road conditions but, for the most part, it was just her.

High above, two eagles soared, using the thermals to gain height without effort. Sheep grazed on the scrubby grass, bees hummed, and birds trilled. Chloe sighed in contentment; this was utter perfection.

2
_____

Chloe ate her picnic in splendid seclusion, perched on a rock, resting against her backpack. Happy in her own company, she whiled away a good couple of hours, content to do nothing but stare at the scenery, and maybe doze a little.

Eventually, collecting her stuff and making sure she left nothing behind, Chloe set off back. She didn't hurry, there was nothing wasting, just her and the evening. While ambling along, she pondered dinner.

There was a new Italian restaurant close by, and you were always guaranteed a good feed at the Salen Hotel, or she could have beans on toast at the cottage. No decision made, she noticed she was almost at the pull-in where she left Bessie — her car.

Loath to leave yet, she strolled down to the water's edge, and stretched her back — unused muscles already beginning to tighten. A multitude of pebbles, flattened smooth by the constant ebb and flow of the water tumbling them together, crunched underfoot and, suddenly, Chloe had an urge to skim them, a favourite pastime.

Intent on improving her skill, it took her several minutes to register a mewling cry. Presuming it to be a late-born lamb calling for its ewe, she ignored it, exchanging the pebble she was holding for her camera, to take her millionth photo of yet another exquisitely formed purple thistle, which caught her eye.

The crying did not abate, in fact, it seemed to become more frantic. Dropping her camera into her backpack, which she slung over her shoulders, Chloe headed in the direction of the sound.

Backtracking a little way, she soon spotted the cause of the plaintive wail; a lamb, apparently stuck in a boggy bit of ground. It wasn't sinking, but it was definitely panicking, and its mother was standing to one side, her head swinging back and forth in distress. At least, Chloe assumed it was distress.

Glancing along the road, there was not a soul around; not a farmer, a walker or even a passing car, and she knew sheep were apt to wander a fair way from their home farm.

Well, she couldn't leave it, who knew when or, more likely, *if* the farmer would happen by. Thankful she was wearing fast drying, three-quarter, hiking pants, Chloe rolled them up as far as possible, removed her walking shoes, and socks, placed her backpack on the mossy ground, then gingerly slid down to the same level as the two sheep.

Cautiously inching closer, Chloe talked soothingly to the lamb hoping to calm its fear, while at the same time telling herself it was a good job none of her colleagues could see her, this would give them a good laugh. Quiet, mousey, staid Chloe up to her armpits in muck trying to rescue a lamb.

Mud squelched around her toes and crawled up her calves; she *really* hoped nothing wriggled around her ankles, there would definitely be screaming if that happened. Reaching the lamb, she stroked its woolly head, shuffling until she could get a purchase on its body. Wrapping her arms around its midriff, Chloe pulled — nothing. She tried again, tried several times — nothing, absolutely nothing.

Dammit, the creature was stuck fast.

. . .

Taking a breather, she pondered her options. The afternoon was almost over, the summer evenings were long, but the air would cool down fairly quickly and Chloe had no intention of leaving the lamb stuck in a bog all night. She could try to flag down a car or drive to the nearest house and hope it was the farm to which the lamb belonged, or she could persevere.

While she didn't think the lamb would get sucked under — she had not sunk any further than her knees — she was concerned it was vulnerable to birds of prey, or foxes — unsure whether there were any of the latter roaming around on Mull.

Gritting her teeth, she tried one more time and, at last, was rewarded by a squelching sound as the bog began to relinquish its hapless victim. Beads of sweat formed on her brow, as she heaved and pulled.

Inch by painful inch the lamb came unstuck, then, without warning, and accompanied by a sort of loud sucking gulp, the lamb was free. The suddenness sent Chloe sprawling, and the lamb rolled on top of her.

With a 'baaaaa' the creature shook itself, and gambolled over to its relieved mother, the pair trotting off along the grass, without so much as a backwards glance.

Chloe was covered from head to toe in smelly mud. There was no way she could get in the car like that. Shivering a little in the breeze, she glanced at the loch. The sun was still on it, and although she knew it would be icy cold, it was better than getting mud on the car seat.

Decision made, she padded across to the shore, and hurriedly stripped down to her lacy underwear. Trying not to yell with shock when the chill water met her overheated skin, she braved the loch and without pausing to think — for to do so would be to retreat — dived under.

A sleek grey car rounded a curve in the road, the driver's eye, catching sight of a head bobbing at the edge of the loch. Thinking it was a seal, the man pulled over to watch for a moment, before grabbing his camera to capture the perfect shot of the marine creature in the late afternoon sunlight.

He was startled, therefore, when the seal stood up and started to wade out of the water. Lowering his camera and shaking his head, sure he was imagining things, the man peered at the figure. It was a woman. A tall, shapely woman, long fair hair streaming across her shoulders, water running down her body in rivulets.

He was mesmerised.

Dominic Winters was a reluctant visitor to Mull. His family owned a holiday house on the island, one they rented out, and, because he happened to be in Oban on business, his mother asked him to check on it.

There was someone due to rent it at the end of July and, despite an eminently professional letting agent handling it, Mrs Winters had a bee in her bonnet. Dominic grudgingly agreed; it was easier than dealing with her complaints if he ignored her.

Arriving on the island that morning, he checked into the Isle of Mull Hotel at Craignure, then decided to take a drive around the island. It was a beautiful day; he might as well enjoy his stay. Tomorrow, he would inspect the house; there was time enough to organise any required repairs.

He took the long way around, passed Duart castle, skirting Loch Spelve and all the way down to Ffionphort. Parking up, Dominic strolled down to the narrow strait separating Mull from Iona, and sitting on a convenient rock, lunched on a doorstop of a beef sandwich and a cup of piping hot coffee.

Under the bright, late spring sunshine and cloudless azure sky, the water between the two islands was turquoise, glimmering in the light breeze. Seagulls wheeled and turned; their keening cry the only sound to shatter the peace. Surprisingly, on so glorious a day, there were few visitors. Dominic, not one for crowds, preferred it this way, and relaxed with his coffee.

Dawdling back along quiet roads, he turned left at the head of Loch Beg, taking the route which loosely circled the lower western slopes of Ben More — the highest peak on Mull — and on towards Gribun Rocks.

By now it was late afternoon, the roads remained empty, and Dominic indulged his passion for photography by stopping here and there to take pictures of the endless views. He was enjoying himself. To have no real responsibilities, even for a brief while, was liberating — a feeling somewhat alien to him.

It was as Dominic cruised along the edge of Loch Na Keal, in the shadow of Gribun, that he spotted what he assumed to be a seal. His mistake had him squinting in disbelief, when a woman rose out of the loch.

Refusing to heed the stories nudging at his brain about selkies, however insistent they were, Dominic lowered his camera a couple of inches and stared unashamedly.

3

She came out of the water and onto the shingle, water pouring off her tall, curvaceous body, which swayed provocatively as she walked, lacy underwear leaving little to the imagination.

Smoothing her hands over her long hair, she brought it over one shoulder and twisted it to squeeze out the excess water, then leaned forward and tossed her head back. Unable to drag his gaze away, Dominic was captivated as her hair formed a perfect arc. Water droplets sprayed out, catching the sunlight, tiny crystals hanging in the air before bursting into a million miniscule bubbles.

In any other circumstance, the scene would look contrived, but this woman seemed entirely unselfconscious and completely unaware she was being observed.

His finger had a mind of its own, and even though his brain screamed *voyeur*, Dominic found himself pressing the camera button at least three times. The term poetry in motion floated through his head while he watched her pick her way, carefully, to a car parked nearby on the grass.

He saw her open the boot and pull out a towel to wrap herself in, then dig out what appeared to be a pair of flip-flops, slipping her feet into them. He was close enough to discern she was shivering. *No surprise there... what on earth possessed her to take a dip in the loch at this time of day?*

A vague sense of concern, impelled Dominic to stow his camera under the seat, and climb out of the car. He sauntered along the verge to the lay-by, his footsteps silent in the grass.

"Is everything okay, miss?" he called on his approach.

The woman jumped, and bit down on a squawk. "Where did you come from?" she demanded. "Creeping up on a person. There's a name for people like you." A fiery stain colouring her cheeks, perhaps recalling her state of undress.

"People like me?" he rejoined, amused. "You mean people who come to check on the well-being of others? Those kinds of people." Conveniently forgetting he had just taken photos of her virtually naked.

"Well... I suppose..." she grumbled, then her manners kicked in. "Thank you, sir. I am fine. I had to rescue a lamb, then I fell in the bog, and it was better to clean off in the loch than drive home coated in stinking mud." Spoken with a nonchalance, that made Dominic ponder whether, for this woman, such things were a common occurrence.

"You're frozen."

"I'll be fine when I get some clothes on." By now the woman's teeth were chattering.

"Well hurry up then, you'll catch your death."

She stared at him pointedly, until he grinned, and very slowly turned his back on her. He could hear rustling noises as she, presumably, rooted around in the boot for something to wear.

He thought that in itself was quite telling. Most people didn't carry a change of clothes in their car, on the off-chance they'd be required. While she sorted herself out, he was content to admire the view.

The sun was beginning its long trek to the horizon, the early evening light becoming slightly hazy. The midges would be out soon. Dominic shuddered; he hated the bloodsucking little buggers.

"Right, I'm decent," her quiet voice broke into his reverie. Turning, he noticed she had pulled on a baggy sweat shirt and a pair of leggings. They did nothing for her, but she didn't seem to care.

"Thank you for stopping to make sure I'm okay. I'm sorry for interrupting your drive." She glanced out over the loch. "Mind you it's so beautiful here, being interrupted is essential. Excuse me while I go and bag up my muddy clothes."

The woman hurried off across the springy turf to the water's edge where her clothes lay in a heap. He watched as she gathered everything together and stuffed them into the plastic bag, she had taken with her. Then, picking up her shoes, she trudged back to the car and dropped the lot into the boot, slamming the lid.

Without knowing what prompted it, Dominic felt the need to extend their acquaintance. He was only here until the day after tomorrow anyway; what harm could it do?

"I wonder, and this is rather presumptuous as you don't know me from Adam but, would you like to join me for a drink?"

The woman gaped at him, looked down at herself, touched her wet hair and brought her gaze back to his.

"Errr... hmmm... why?" she asked, obviously puzzled. "I'm not exactly dressed for it and there's a fair chance I still have mud stuck in places I do not care to think about." Frowning when she realised how personal that sounded. "Sorry, that was probably oversharing," she shifted uncomfortably, hot colour drifting back up her face.

Dominic chuckled. He couldn't help it. "Good afternoon, my name is Dominic Winters, and I'm only on Mull for a couple of days. My family owns property hereabouts and my mother asked me to check on it. I am thirty-six years old and am the estate manager at Lanchester Hall. I promise you I have no nefarious intent." He paused.

"There, you know quite a lot about me. Please join me for a drink. I am here on my own, and I do believe I would enjoy your company."

Oh, so he believed he would enjoy her company, did he? Did he think he was doing her some kind of favour? Taking pity on the clumsy idiot who fell into the bog? Well pooh to that. Determined to say no, Chloe was appalled when she heard herself accept his invitation. *Dammit.* Nothing she could do about it now, so she responded in kind.

"Pleased to meet you. My name is Chloe Shepherd, and I am on Mull for a whole month." Unable to stop from smiling as she said this, transforming her rather ordinary face. "I have a boring office job and, while I cannot imagine I am someone who attracts those with nefarious intent, I am relieved to know you are not among them."

She sucked in a breath. It was a long speech for a woman who preferred to keep conversation to a minimum. Something about this man made her mouth and brain refuse to behave sensibly.

Dominic watched the woman as she spoke, and felt his brow creasing at her words, but couldn't think why. Ignoring it for now, he said. "How about we meet in, say an hour, at the Salen Hotel? Will that give you time to... errr... remove any last vestiges of bog?"

Chloe rummaged in her backpack and withdrew her phone, the screen said it was coming up to half five. "That sounds great, if you are sure." she said, hesitantly, confused as to why he wanted to prolong what was nothing more than a check on her well-being.

"I am quite sure," he affirmed, and set off towards his car. "See you soon." He threw this last casually over his shoulder and Chloe just nodded, abstractedly, forgetting he was facing the other way.

Not hearing her reply, Dominic glanced around, spotting her silent acknowledgement, and smiled. *This could be an interesting diversion.*

4

Chloe closed the boot and climbed into her own vehicle, where she just sat, lost in thought. Random invitations to have a drink with a man never happened to her. She was far too shy and rarely went out with the crowd from work. She felt awkward in large groups of people; acutely aware she was usually invited out of pity, or to make up the numbers. It wasn't necessary, she was perfectly happy in her own company.

Pulling herself together, Chloe switched on the engine and turned up the heater, feeling the warmth begin to take the chill out of her body. Reversing the car, she turned around and rolled forward, pausing at the edge of the grass to check for oncoming cars.

An expensive-looking grey car rolled past, gathering pace, a hand waved, and she waved back without thinking, then realised it was Dominic. She eased out and followed him, but he was going at quite a lick, his tail lights disappearing almost before she was up to the speed limit.

Shaking her head at his recklessness, Chloe drove at a far more sedate pace. Sheep or cattle, completely devoid of any road sense, were a common occurrence along this route, and she had no desire to hit either.

It wasn't long before she was parking behind the cottage. Hooking her backpack over one shoulder and heaving the bag containing her filthy clothes out of the boot, Chloe locked the car and traipsed indoors. Dumping the clothes into the laundry sink, she dropped the backpack on one of the chairs and headed for the bathroom.

Standing under the shower, luxuriating in the heat from the powerful spray, Chloe's mind wandered back to Dominic Winters, trying and failing to work out why he asked her to meet him for a drink. She came to the conclusion he probably felt sorry for her getting all muddy and was maybe bored with his own company.

Mentally shrugging, she shampooed her hair and scrubbed away any bog residue with a thoroughness that left her skin tingling. After towelling off, she dried her hair, and twisted it into a loose bun.

Slipping into three-quarter jeans and a dark green V-necked, long sleeved T-shirt, she studied herself in the mirror. She frowned a little at the reflection staring back at her. It didn't matter how long she looked, it wouldn't change. Pulling a grotesque face, she went downstairs.

Emptying her backpack, Chloe carried the containers and flask she used for her picnic into the kitchen and washed them, leaving them on the drainer to air dry. Then she removed the battery from her camera, and set it charging, before retrieving her purse and phone, and tucking them into her handbag.

At the door, Chloe remembered something and retraced her steps. Going into the tiny laundry, she filled the sink with water, hoping a long soak would help dislodge caked-on mud. Grinning as the water changed from clear to dirty brown, she turned off the tap, glanced around to make sure everything was at it should be, and left.

Being relatively early in the evening, the Salen Hotel was not too busy, and when she walked in, Chloe spotted Dominic. He was already sitting at a table by the window, overlooking the rear garden and beyond to the Sound.

For a split second, she questioned her decision to have a drink with a man she didn't know, contemplating whether to turn tail. As the thought filtered through her mind, he twisted in his seat and, seeing her hovering at the door, smiled. It was a slow, gentle smile, friendly and open. Chloe's feet moved towards him, even as her head warned her to be wary, he was far too good-looking — dangerously so.

He stood when she reached the table, to pull out her chair. She thanked him and sat down, dropping her bag on the floor and admiring the view, one of which she never tired.

"What would you like to drink?" Dominic asked, taking his wallet out of his back pocket.

"Oh, a glass of rosé, please. I think that's the perfect reward for saving a lamb." She grinned, and Dominic went over to the bar, returning moments later with their respective drinks.

He resumed his seat and the two, after a brief and slightly awkward silence, began to talk. Without seeming to, Dominic learnt quite a bit about Chloe Shepherd, who in turn discovered why Dominic Winters was on Mull.

"My mother wants me to run my eye over a property we own on the island. It's vacant at the moment, so it's a good opportunity to make sure everything is in working order. To be fair, the agents have never let us down but for some reason Mum wants a family member to inspect it periodically. I think it's because my grandparents used to live there."

He shrugged, still perplexed by his mother's request. "I just happened to be in Oban for a couple of days, so I drew the short straw."

"Not a bad idea," Chloe remarked. "I expect families spot things even the most rigorous inspection by a letting agent will miss. You know what to look for when it's your own home. Plus, surely coming here could never be considered the short straw. I mean just look at that."

She nodded towards the panorama in front of them; the Sound, sparkling under the evening sunshine, and beyond to the Hills of Morven, smoky shadows in the far distance.

"I suppose, but I was only supposed to be away from the estate for a couple of days, not the week it'll end up being. Mum seems to think I can just divert here on her whim. You're right though, the view *is* pretty awesome. I tend to forget." He grinned, and they both fell quiet, lost in contemplation.

"Let's order before the hordes descend," Chloe suggested, glancing at her watch. By seven the pub would be full, and she was pretty hungry. Dominic agreed, the comfortable silence lengthening while they perused the menu.

"I think I'll have scampi and chips with salad." Chloe decided. "I'm on holiday and it's my favourite. Do you know what you fancy?"

"I'll go with the fish."

Chloe stood. "I'll order, shall I? I think we can open a tab."

Dominic nodded his agreement, thinking how refreshing it was to be with a woman who wanted an actual meal rather than worrying about how many calories there were in a lettuce leaf.

5

Over the meal the two chatted about this and that. Their conversation flowed easily, considering they had known each other for less than half an hour, especially when they realised they shared similar interests.

They both loved books, history, photography, solitude, stargazing, Scotland, whisky, good coffee, and walking, to name a few. Meal eaten, they relaxed over another glass of wine for Chloe, and, because he was driving, a tonic water for Dominic.

Soon, however, their respective days caught up with them, neither able to prevent yawns.

"Much as I have enjoyed this evening, I think I need to call it a night, and you don't want to be falling asleep behind the wheel." Chloe said with a grin.

Refusing to accept any money from Chloe, Dominic paid their tab. "I invited you, my treat," he stated and, after thanking the bartender, the pair strolled out to the carpark.

Dominic offered to walk Chloe home. She assured him she was just along the street and would be fine. She didn't know him and, despite the sense of trust she felt when with him, leading him right to her door was something she not prepared to do. She had watched far too many murder mysteries.

"I have to see this rental property tomorrow morning, but would you fancy meeting me in Tobermory for lunch?" Dominic asked as they said goodnight.

"I think that would be lovely," Chloe smiled, and Dominic felt an unaccustomed heat flicker through him. She was really quite beautiful.

"I look forward to it, say twelve?"

"Sounds great, see you then." Chloe waved as she walked off in the dusk, vanishing around the corner.

Dominic watched until she was out of sight, wondering how such an unexpected encounter could possibly leave so profound an impression.

Shaking his head, he got into the car and followed the winding road back to his hotel.

The next day, Dominic was up and breakfasted early. He wanted to do this inspection and then drive over to Tobermory for a potter before meeting Chloe.

His dad had asked him to pop into the island's distillery, located on the harbour, to buy a bottle or two of their Ledaig. Named for what used to be the hamlet next to Tobermory, it was his father's favourite whisky.

Plan made, Dominic checked to be sure he had the keys to the cottage, then grabbed his wallet and jacket — it might be early June, but the mornings could be cool.

The drive along the Sound was glorious. Dominic wound down the window, inhaling the soft Scottish air. The sun was sparkling on the placid water, seagulls wheeled overhead, and the roads were quiet. It was just after nine-thirty. The rush hour, if there was such a thing here on Mull, was long over and it was still early enough in the season that the tourist buses were less frequent.

Dominic felt suddenly light of heart, along with a sense of anticipation, although about what he wasn't sure. Halfway there, he pulled in to the side of the road and got out. Stretching his back to loosen muscles still niggling from long hours driving over the last couple of days, he stood for several moments and just soaked it in.

To his right Duart Castle — the seat of Clan Maclean — jutted out into the Sound, its imposing outline instantly recognisable to movie buffs. To his left, Fishnish, complete with a ferry on final approach. In front, mainland Scotland, where the distant mountains — subdued greenish-brown in the morning sunlight — seemed to float.

It was several years since Dominic last visited Mull, but he felt its magic seeping into his bones. There was something indefinably special about this island. He could never pinpoint it and if asked, would have rejected it as nonsense, but today, in the tranquility, surrounded by such astonishing beauty, he acknowledged the truth of it.

Grinning at his poetic turn of mind, he drew another deep breath, then got back in the car and drove the last few miles to Salen. He pulled around the back of the cottage, frowning when he noticed another car in the allocated spot.

Irritated that people thought it was acceptable to take up a space clearly marked for tenants only, he made a mental note to mention it to the letting agent. It would not look very professional if a guest arrived and found they could not park because someone decided to ignore the sign.

Then he noticed the washing line; it had clothes pegged out along its length. *Really? How rude! Who on earth was cheeky enough to use someone else's washing line?* Such inconsiderate behaviour was unheard of on Mull.

Sliding the key into the lock, Dominic pushed open the door and let it swing closed behind him. Walking into the kitchen, he came to an abrupt standstill.

What the hell?

Standing in the middle of the table was a cup of something hot, given the steam hovering above it. Glancing around, he saw signs of habitation: an upturned glass on the drainer, a backpack on the floor by the laundry door, and the smell of toast tickled his nostrils.

What the hell?

Yanking his phone out of his pocket, he searched his contact list for the agent's number. He would call them, and then the local police. He was on hold for the agent when he heard footsteps on the wooden stairs and... *was that humming? Did squatters hum?* Why not? They'd be very happy to find free and very comfortable accommodation.

Hanging up, Dominic folded his arms, plastered a scowl on his face, and waited.

Chloe woke to the sound of birds trilling outside her bedroom window. Squinting at the bedside clock, she groaned when she saw it was barely six. Rolling over, she tried to snatch another hour or so, but it was hopeless, she was wide awake.

Tutting in frustration, she got up. After rinsing off her clothes, still soaking in the laundry sink, and putting them in the washing machine, she went for a long walk, an hour passing as though a mere moment.

Back at the cottage, Chloe hung out the washing, and decided she was hungry enough to have breakfast before she showered. Three slices of toast and two cups of tea later, she felt refreshed and ready to face anything.

After a quick shower, Chloe wrapped herself in one of the huge towels and went down to the kitchen to brew a strong coffee, thinking to drink it in the garden. Placing the steaming mug on the table, she hurried back upstairs to get dressed.

Shrugging into her clothes, she hummed to herself while descending the stairs. Entering the kitchen, she let out a shriek of fright. A tall shadow lurking in the doorway moved towards her.

Squeezing her eyes shut, because clearly *that* would induce an intruder to leave her alone, Chloe yelled. "Get out, get out, get out, or I'm calling the police." Forgetting her phone was upstairs.

"What in blazes are you doing in my house?" a deep voice bellowed at the same time.

Then...

"*Chloe?*"

She recognised that voice. *It couldn't be?* She risked a peek. *Bloody bugger and sod, it was!* It was Dominic.

"*Dominic?*" Trembling with shock, she gaped at the man she met the day before, trying to work out why he was in her kitchen. Unbidden, his remark from the previous afternoon filtered into her head. He was here to inspect a property. Typical — it would have to be the one she was renting.

His sudden appearance seemed to have robbed Chloe of coherence, so rather than gabble unintelligibly, she grabbed the coffee and swallowed it in three gulps, hoping the caffeine might snap her back into gear.

6

Dominic could not decide who was more startled. One look at Chloe's face confirmed it was definitely her. She was staring at him as though he had grown two heads. The car and washing made much more sense now.

"God, I am so sorry, Chloe," he hastened to apologise. "I was given to understand the cottage was empty. Mum said it wasn't due to be rented 'til the end of July."

"It was a last-minute decision. I only booked a couple of weeks ago." Chloe slumped into the closest chair, heart still thudding, her legs a bit wobbly. "Errr... well I... suppose you should check whatever it is you have to check." She waved her hand, distract-edly. "Coffee, I need another coffee. Want one?"

"That would be lovely," Dominic replied, hiding a grin when she made no attempt to move. "Shall I?"

"What... no, I'm fine, just give me a sec," she said, willing her legs to stop quaking.

"It's no problem, I know where the coffee pot is. Plus, as it's my fault you are a bit shaken up, I feel it's only fair," he paused. "Better still, how about we go out for one? I can do the checklist later. I think fresh air and coffee is far more important right now."

He smiled encouragingly, and Chloe heard herself agreeing. That was the second time in less than twenty-four hours — honestly, no wonder her Aunt Meg worried about her.

"I should get my jacket," she muttered, and stumped back up the stairs, pleased to note her legs were working almost normally.

Shortly thereafter, they were motoring towards Tobermory.

"I know this will delay coffee but once we're there we can relax." Dominic explained.

Chloe nodded and admired the view. The windows were down, and the breeze whipped through her hair, tugging strands from the tidy plait she had fashioned it into. Chloe didn't seem bothered.

Dominic, who found himself glancing across at her more often than would be considered polite, was fascinated. All that hair in his face would drive him bonkers.

Dominic edged the car, expertly, into a narrow parking space near the Tobermory Visitor's Centre. The bay was like a mill pond, reflecting the colourful houses circling its edge. Chloe couldn't help herself, and snapped a few more pictures using her phone, pinging one of them to her aunt.

"This view never gets old," she sighed contentedly. "I would never leave if I lived here."

"Ahhh, but it's not so enjoyable in the middle of winter, when the storms blow through. Brrrr... it's far less welcoming then.

"Yes, but can you imagine curling up in front of a roaring fire, nursing a large dram of whisky, listening to the gale howling around and the rain lashing at the windows, knowing you are snug and safe inside?"

Dominic stared at Chloe.

Her words conjured up an image of her bundled up in winter gear trudging through thick snow. Her shining hair tumbling out from under a woolly hat, laughing as they carried chopped wood into a cosy room, lit by the glow from the fire on which they were about to place the kindling. Two glasses of amber nectar side-by-side on a little table, waiting to take the chill out of their veins.

Wait... they carried wood... two glasses? No, this was not his vision, it was Chloe's. Even as he thought it, a most peculiar yearning to be part of the scene, nudged at Dominic's subconscious. Mentally he shook it off. He was here for another day, tops. Definitely not enough time to be thinking about such things, irresistible though they were.

"Right, coffee." Dragging his mind back to the matter at hand, Dominic pointed to one of the tearooms along the harbour. "They serve the most amazing cakes, home-baked every morning." He said as he led the way.

It didn't take long to reach the tearoom and order. Chloe decided on a piece of coffee and walnut cake, while Dominic chose the lemon slice.

The coffee, when it arrived, was dark and rich, just the way Chloe liked it and, closing her eyes, she took a deep breath, letting the heady aroma swirl around her senses.

"Bliss," she announced and took a sip. "Ooof, hot though." Sucking air into her mouth in an effort to cool it, the gesture making Dominic chuckle.

"Well, duh, what did you expect? It's just come out of the coffee maker at a gazillion degrees."

"Exaggerating much?" she grinned. For a little while they bantered back and forth, but soon conversation, quite naturally, turned to their lives. Chloe was interested in knowing more about Dominic's job.

"I didn't think there were such things as estate managers any more. Didn't that job title die out years ago?"

"How do you suppose stately homes still in private hands cope without them?" Dominic rejoined, raising a quizzical brow. "Even those owned by groups like the National Trust and English Heritage require some form of stewardship. Flora and fauna don't always look after themselves you know." His tone gently chiding.

"Sorry, I guess if I'd thought about it, I would have realised. Hadn't really occurred to me. I mean, I love visiting those kinds of places, I just never considered what goes on behind the scenes. Mind, I did watch the program about Chatsworth, that was amazing, so interesting." She chattered on in this vein for a while then asked, "So what's Lanchester Hall like?"

Chloe listened attentively, while Dominic talked about his job. It was clear he loved his work. How wonderful, to look forward to your daily tasks. She hated hers. Yes, she was competent enough, but it was mind-numbing.

Her mind wandered momentarily, as she pictured her life had she found work in a museum or at one of the historical sites scattered around Britain.

Dominic watched as Chloe's expression, in a split-second, morphed from cheerful to remote and pondered the cause. She seemed far away from a pleasant tearoom in Tobermory.

"Chloe?" No response, "Chloe?" He put his hand over hers, intending to bring her out of her introspection, when a curious sensation trickled up his arm. Like a kind of effervescence.

He jerked his hand back, assuming it was just static, then tried again. This time there was no weird tingle, and he shook her hand slightly. Her eyes refocused on him, a question in their dove-grey hue.

"Sorry, I kind of drifted off there. How rude of me. Did I miss something?"

"No, but you suddenly looked sad, and I was puzzled as to the reason."

Chloe studied Dominic, wondering why he cared? He was only on the island until tomorrow. She indulged in moment's scrutiny. To her, Dominic was unconventionally handsome — by which she meant he didn't have the film star good looks that people seemed to swoon over.

He was tall, and powerfully built, with angular features, slightly shaggy dark blonde hair, and eyes an interesting shade — somewhere between hazel and green. What a shame he would be leaving so soon, he was the sort of man she would like to get to know.

Then she dismissed the notion. He could well be engaged, married, certainly he must be dating, he was far too handsome to be single. Her shoulders drooped a little, then she took hold of herself and straightened up.

"I was just thinking how delightful it must be to love your job," she explained.

"You don't love yours?"

"Lord, no. I'm an admin clerk in an assessors' office. The only plus about my job is that I don't have to people at all."

"You don't have to *people*? What does that mean?"

"Interact with the public face-to-face. I do everything via telephone and email. The only people I ever meet are our mechanics, who are a great bunch, thankfully." She shrugged. "To have a job you look forward to doing everyday. I can only imagine."

"If you had your choice, what would you want to do?"

"Anything connected with history, the more ancient, the better," came the immediate reply.

"And why..."

"Because such jobs are rare. Ever since the telly started broadcasting those fascinating history programs, everyone wants to work in that discipline. There are no openings and any that come up have hundreds of applicants. You'd think having parents in the field both academically and literally, would count for something... nope. So, I turn up, do my job and leave. The only bonus being I earned enough to save a little and to come here for a month."

7

"Your parents?" Dominic quizzed.

"Yeah, they're archaeologists, working on a dig somewhere"

"Would I have heard of them? My brother-in-law is an archaeologist, and I hear plenty of names bandied about when he and my sister get started on one of their debates." His tone was one of good-humoured resignation.

"Hmmm... maybe, they are quite eminent..." she trailed off.

Dominic couldn't understand why she sounded so hesitant. "Come on, Chloe, spill," he encouraged, surprised to see a slight curl of her lip and a shadow over her eyes. "Chloe?"

She looked at him steadily for what seemed an age then kind of huffed. "Greg and Alison Shepherd."

Dominic's jaw dropped. She *had* to be kidding him. He was a bit of a history buff and an avid viewer of the aforementioned documentaries on the subject. Alison and Greg Shepherd appeared in many of them, their expertise undeniable — their on-screen personas, genial, open and friendly.

A glance at Chloe's face told him it was no joke. Dominic studied her, trying and failing to see any resemblance.

"Are you sure... God, sorry what am I saying, of course you're sure. It's just..." he paused, unwilling to voice his thoughts.

"... how could such a boring, plain Jane be the daughter of such clever, vivacious, and beautiful people?" Chloe finished for him her voice, flat. "Yeah, because that's *never* been a question I've been asked before." Annoyed with herself for allowing old insecurities to niggle.

Every damn time she mentioned her parents it was the same, so she rarely told anyone any more. Despite knowing him only a brief time, Chloe had gained the impression Dominic wasn't like most people. She hoped she hadn't read him wrong, although did it really matter? He would be gone in less than twenty-four hours.

"Hey, that's not what I was about to say," Dominic countered. "I was going to say how come you ended up in a job you hate when it's clear you love history and, are you sure your parents are not interested in helping you?"

"Even if they were interested, I don't want their help. I don't want anything from them." Chloe almost spat the words, fighting to curb her anger. She closed her eyes and counted to ten, then did it again. By the third time, she was back in control.

"I apologise. I overreacted, it's... habit I suppose." She twisted her fingers together, then drew another weighty sigh. "My parents don't know me, at all..."

At Dominic's raised brow, she swallowed her customary reserve and gave him a condensed version of her childhood, just enough to clarify her response to his comment.

There was silence when she finished speaking. Dominic, who understood more from what she didn't say than what she did, was almost overcome with the most inconvenient urge to kiss her right there in the tearoom.

Probably not the best idea, but there was just something about Chloe, she elicited emotions he didn't think he possessed.

Maybe it was the hint of vulnerability, one she hid under a veneer of casual cheerfulness.

Maybe it was her beautiful grey eyes, maybe it was her glimmering hair, or that body he had been privileged enough to see almost naked — heat coiling through him at the picture in his head.

"I get it. Truly I do. My boss, well she was my boss, kind of still is... it's a bit complicated — I'll explain one day — anyway, her parents treated her appallingly, and most people didn't even know she existed. It took her years to come to terms with their behaviour, to realise it was their issue not hers. She still struggles occasionally but is now surrounded by people whose unconditional love and support have helped boost her self-worth enormously."

Dominic smiled in reminiscence. Alex Faulkner, who at 29, bore the lofty title of Countess of Lanchester, was not only his sort of boss, she was also his sister's best friend. He and his family had known her all her life, witness to the consequences wrought by parents who had absolutely no interest whatsoever in their daughter.

Although the circumstances differed to a degree, he knew Alex would understand and empathise with Chloe. It also made Dominic truly grateful, he belonged to a loving family.

Chloe heard the 'I'll explain one day,' and, even accepting it was a throw away comment, it made her feel warm all over. She glanced at her watch. "Do you fancy a stroll along the harbour before lunch, that is, if you still want to bother with lunch since we had coffee."

"Sounds great and, of course, I want to have lunch with you. Come on." Dominic paid for their coffee and cakes, refusing to accept anything from Chloe towards it, "nope, I suggested meeting for coffee, my shout," and they were out in the sunshine.

They walked along, chatting about this and that and at some

point, Chloe realised Dominic had hooked her arm through his. Despite their short acquaintance, it felt oddly fitting — more than friends, but not as intimate as holding hands. Unwilling to query it, she just enjoyed the contact.

Ambling along the harbour, they stopped here and there to take a photo or pop into one of the little shops. As they turned at the far end of the road, where the Kilchoan ferry came in, Dominic suggested they drive around to Dervaig for lunch.

"We've spent the morning here, so why don't we try somewhere else for lunch?"

"That sounds lovely, but are you sure? I don't want to take up all your day."

"Why not?"

"Well... don't you have anything better to do, than hang with me?"

"Nothing pressing, unless I'm boring you."

"No, no, that's not what I meant, it's just... oh bugger..." Chloe clamped her mouth shut.

Dominic chuckled. "I'm winding you up. Chloe Shepherd, I am enjoying your company. Please join me for lunch at Dervaig, then maybe we could go onto Calgary and walk along the beach."

"Okay, okay, I give in." Chloe grinned and lifted her hands in capitulation. "To be honest, that sounds fabulous. There's the most amazing cafe, just outside Dervaig. It's up a lane on the opposite side of the road, if it's still there. It serves the best food. Hmmmm... can't remember the name... wait... I think it might be The Old Byre..."

"The Old Byre." Dominic said, at the same time. "Yes, it's still there. Right, that's sorted, let's go." He tucked her arm through his again.

Resuming, what was swiftly becoming, effortless conversation, they retraced their steps along the bustling harbour, and to outward appearances, looked to have known each other for years.

Following a brief diversion to the distillery, so Dominic could buy the whisky for his father, they were motoring towards Dervaig.

8

Soon, they were perusing the menu at The Old Byre, both choosing Crofters Soup, a hearty broth which came with a great hunk of freshly baked bread. While waiting for it to be prepared, Chloe pottered about the gift shop, several items catching her eye. She didn't need anything, but it was nice to splurge now and again, and she wanted to take something back for Aunt Meg.

The food arrived and conversation dwindled while they ate. The soup was filling but, as he had been the evening before, Dominic was gratified to see Chloe wipe the remnants from the bottom of the bowl with her last chunk of bread.

"Oh, that was sooooo good." Chloe clutched her stomach. "I am so full I don't think I'll be able to move for at least an hour," she groaned, folding her serviette and placing it neatly alongside the bowl. "I could eat that every day and never get sick of it. Yum!"

"Agreed, so how about we have a cup of tea and let it digest?"

"I like your thinking." Chloe smiled, and Dominic felt that same peculiar sensation ripple through him. He forced it back. He was leaving tomorrow, studiously ignoring the slight tightening in his chest at the thought. He just had to make today last.

By the time they reached Calgary, the afternoon was half over, but that meant the majority of tourists had already left. This was one of Chloe's favourite spots on Mull, and she had spent many happy hours here on previous visits. Just beyond the tiny hamlet, nestled in a sheltered dip, lay Calgary Beach.

The soft, brilliant-white sand, turquoise sea and cloudless blue sky was a photographer's dream. Chloe retrieved her digital camera from her backpack and took numerous pictures. The light breeze had created a gentle swell, and the sun sparkling on the waves was magical.

The pair walked the length of the beach and, on the way back, Chloe, unable to stop herself, slipped off her shoes so she could paddle. Dominic shouldered her backpack, and grabbed her shoes, tying them together by the laces.

"You go paddle, I'll find somewhere to sit. No rush." He grinned at her childlike enthusiasm, and wandered to the top of the beach, seeking out a suitable rock.

Perching on his chosen ledge, Dominic leaned back, relishing the opportunity to observe Chloe uninterrupted. She had rolled up her jeans, but they were already damp. She was kicking through the shallows, sending streams of water into the air, the crystal-like droplets reminding Dominic of the previous afternoon. *Was it only yesterday?* It was as though he had known her for ever.

While he watched, Dominic came to the conclusion he did not want to go home the next day. He wanted the chance to discover whether these feelings he was beginning to experience had any substance, or whether they were all in his head... or a much lower part of his anatomy, which inconveniently throbbed at the mere idea of prolonging his time with Chloe.

Good grief, I'm worse than a horny teenager, he thought, shifting the backpack to cover his swelling flesh. Closing his eyes,

Dominic summoned up images of his grandmother and his mother, the elderly shopkeeper in the village where he grew up, relieved when his body returned to normal.

Digging out his phone, he rang his office, frowning when he realised the mobile signal was weak here. He tried emailing and texting, with no luck. Hoping both would go as soon as he was in range, he didn't delete either and made a mental note to call as soon as he was able.

Chloe splashed through the breakers, uncaring that the cuffs of her jeans were now thoroughly soaked. Her eyes devoured the view, but her mind was on the man currently getting comfortable on an odd-shaped rock.

She had met him less than twenty-four hours ago. How on earth could he have such an impact on her in so short a time? It was impossible. She did not believe in insta-love. Turning her head slightly, she studied him more or less covertly. He was far enough away not to notice her scrutiny.

His long frame settled on the makeshift seat, his eyes hidden behind dark sunglasses, his unruly hair lifting in the breeze. She noticed him shuffle her backpack and wondered why he didn't stand it on the ground next to him if it was heavy.

What a shame he was going home so soon. It would have been lovely to see whether this... whatever 'this' might be... was simply an enjoyable interlude or something more. *Nothing you can do, Chloe Shepherd,* she instructed herself, while debating whether — since he was leaving anyway — she dared kiss him.

Determined not to let the afternoon go to waste, she made her way back up the beach to where Dominic waited. He seemed to be dozing, so she curled up on the grass, content to admire the scenery.

"Finished paddling?" His quiet question startled her.

"Sorry, thought you were snoozing, I didn't mean to disturb you."

"Too late," he murmured in undertones.

"Beg pardon?"

Unwilling to clarify her disturbing him had nothing to do with waking him from a doze, Dominic replied, "You didn't, I wasn't asleep. Ready to drive on?"

While her head yelled, *No, I want to stay here with you until it's dark, when, under the moonlight, you might be persuaded to kiss me* — her mouth said, "Sure, whenever you're ready."

Dominic unfolded himself from the rock and stood, holding out a hand to pull her up. She grasped it — a faint tingle danced along her arm. She stared at her hand and then up at Dominic who seemed unaffected.

Shaking her head and blaming the enchantment of the isle, she got to her feet. They came face-to-face, so close she could see the bay mirrored in his hazel eyes. Chloe could not look away, mesmerised by the ever-changing hue.

For his part, Dominic was transfixed. He could see himself reflected in the fathomless grey of Chloe's eyes. He didn't want to tear his gaze away, but he really wanted to kiss her.

Did he dare? Surely if she wasn't interested, she would not still be holding his hand. He risked a slight squeeze, a thrill running through him when she responded in kind.

All was peaceful. The tranquil sounds of nature barely penetrated the consciousness of the couple staring at each other, who might as well have been in another world.

Determined not to ruin anything, Dominic whispered. "Chloe..."

"Yes?"

"Would you be offended if I kissed you?"

"Hell, no," her emphatic respond making him chuckle.

"Thank God for that." He cupped the back of her neck. He could feel her plait resting against the back of his hand, it was like a braid of heavy silk and, involuntarily, he entwined it through his fingers.

Bending his head, Dominic grazed his lips against hers, hearing a gentle sigh when their mouths met. Leisurely, he deepened their kiss and, feeling Chloe move closer, released her hand to wrap his arm around her.

His heart rate rocketed when she stepped into him, shaping herself to his tall frame. His whole body trembled with an unexpected onslaught of emotions, and he found himself fighting the urge to strip her naked and make love to her right there on the pristine white beach.

Only the fact it was a public space and he really didn't want to freak Chloe out, prevented him.

9

Chloe was astonished when Dominic asked if she *minded* him kissing her. It was a first, and she rather liked his old-fashioned approach. Ignoring the rational side of her which insisted this was a waste of time, he was leaving, and she would never see him again, Chloe embraced her sentimental nature which would happily have let him kiss her until the end of time. *Who needed moonlight?*

She had only been kissed a few times, casual encounters usually after a night out with uni friends — none amounting to anything more serious. At the time, she was left feeling a bit sad and lonely, thinking how wonderful it would be to be with a guy for longer than an evening.

No strings were all well and good while she was studying, but not much changed when she started work — all the guys she knew *just wanted to be friends*... ugh, she came to hate that phrase.

Presuming she was not cut out for love; Chloe gave up trying. Hence her Aunt Meg's concern — how would her beloved niece meet a 'forever someone' if the only people she ever spent more than half an hour with, were the elderly?

Pushing all that aside, Chloe focused on the moment, savouring every sensation as it washed over her, imprinting each one in her brain so she could recall them when he'd gone.

The temptation to rip off his clothes was almost overwhelming. The only thing stopping her — open beach aside — was that she had never had sex, or even seen a man completely naked before, and had no desire for Dominic to know this. Twenty-six-year-old virgins were probably on the endangered list — it would be laughable if it wasn't so pathetic.

Chloe had no idea how long they kissed until a voice, full of amusement, yelled, 'Get a room.' Hot colour flooding her cheeks, she jerked away, and tried to wriggle out of Dominic's grasp.

"He's only jealous," Dominic murmured in her ear, refusing to let her go.

"Doubtful," she muttered, so quietly, Dominic wasn't sure she actually spoke.

He was perplexed by her reaction. Chloe was quite the paradox. Gorgeous, with a body that went on and on, funny and intelligent. In all honesty, he couldn't understand how she was still single — yet her curious responses indicated a lack of self-confidence and a naiveté unusual these days. He leaned away and studied her face, which still burned from embarrassment.

"Say what now?" he asked.

"Nothing. Never mind. Come on, time we left." Giving him a bright smile, she escaped his hold and, picking up her backpack, set off to the carpark at a brisk pace.

Dominic followed more slowly, mulling over her words.

Chloe Shepherd intrigued him more than any woman he had ever met. He recalled Kassie, his sister, telling him about when she met Gabriel, the man who was now her husband. The circumstances were not the best, but he had never left her thoughts and, although it was two years before they saw each other again, when they did, she realised she had actually fallen in love with him at first sight — something, until then, she always declared to be totally preposterous.

Dominic pondered whether that was what was happening here. Was he falling in love with Chloe? Or was it simply lust? Maybe he should leave. It was a tough call. On the one hand, spending more time with Chloe ought to help him decide — love or lust. On the other, what if it was the latter, but got out of control? He would end up hurting Chloe, and that wasn't fair. *Bugger...!* Never mind what he wanted, what did Chloe want?

Frowning, and no closer to an answer, he unlocked the car and opened the passenger door for Chloe. After dropping her backpack in the boot, she thanked him politely, and slid into the seat.

He couldn't tell what Chloe was thinking. Although, her usual cheerful self, something had changed. Sighing inwardly, he tried not to let it bother him and kept up a flow of chatter.

As the car ate up the miles around the coast, up over the moor and along the undulating road leading to Gruline at the head of Loch Na Keal, he was relieved to notice Chloe had relaxed.

Chloe, that odd moment seemingly forgotten, begged him to stop several times so she could take photos — a request Dominic happily granted. About halfway, he pulled into the tiny parking area near Eas Fors, a spectacular waterfall, and a definite photo opportunity.

After snapping the requisite dozen pictures, the pair stood on the grassy incline, high above the loch, to marvel at the dramatically beautiful scenery. To their right in the distance, the Treshnish Isles — indistinct in the afternoon sunshine. In front of them, nestled Ulva, and Gometra, and to their left Eorsa. Chloe loved the names, they evoked ancient lore, myth, and legend.

Here, in the still of the afternoon — the air redolent with the scent of bracken and peat, the waterfall gurgling behind them —

no sounds of modern life to shatter the peace, the past seemed close enough to touch.

Chloe, with her vivid imagination, could almost see the ghosts of Scottish warriors gathering for a skirmish; or a laird, strolling along the loch, arm in arm with his lady. All going about their daily business as though they still lived.

Dominic, as casually as possible, slung his arm around Chloe.

Without thinking, Chloe rested her head on his shoulder.

The magic of Mull was weaving its spell.

Too soon, they were back on the road, the afternoon nearly over, and Dominic still had to do the inspection, or at least a quick walk through, to satisfy his mother's concerns.

"Would you mind if I do the check when I drop you off?" He broached the subject with Chloe as they passed Gruline.

"'Course not. I'll make a cuppa while you're doing that, or I can even offer you a glass of wine." Chloe, who was swiping through her photos, grinned up at him. "I've got some awesome shots here, they'd make great postcards, or even greeting cards. I'm quite chuffed with myself."

She lifted the camera so he could glance at the image. It was a highland cow, her calf next to her with the sea in the background. Along with the stag, this was probably the archetypal image of the Scottish Highlands.

"Wow, that's stunning, the colours are amazing." Dominic agreed, then a thought struck him. "Why don't you do that?"

"What?"

"Make postcards, or greeting cards?"

"Don't be daft, there's way too many companies already doing that."

"Maybe so, but people are always looking for that unique

image. So many of them are the same shot, from several different angles. If you produced them yourself and started small you could probably get the local businesses here to stock them. It would be great excuse to gallivant around the isles..." he left that dangling while he concentrated on negotiating one of the trickier corners — a blind bend on a rise.

When he looked back at Chloe, she was staring into space, her mouth hanging open ever-so slightly. He smiled to himself. His suggestion might come to nothing, but he recalled her earlier comment about hating her job. This could be just the nudge she needed to start thinking about a change.

10

Ten minutes steady driving and they were coming to a halt at the rear of the cottage. Dominic, as seemed to be his habit, opened the car door for Chloe, and carried her bag indoors. Setting it on the kitchen table, he went back to the car to collect the checklist.

Chloe busied herself making a pot of tea and was about to dig about in the pantry for some biscuits, when she remembered she had dips, crackers, and at least one large bag of crisps. Far more interesting than ginger biccies.

Dominic inspected the cottage with a speed that would have raised his mother's eyebrows. He was thorough, however, and as he suspected, it was well-maintained, the previous renters appeared to have looked after the house with great care. His mother was worrying about nothing.

While he was checking the bathroom, Dominic heard his phone ping and paused to see whether it was an indication his email and message had gone. It was actually a reply, and he allowed himself a smile of triumph when he read it. A week. Perfect.

After trudging back down the stairs, he stuck his head around the kitchen door. No sign of Chloe.

Her, 'I'm here,' floated along the hall from the lounge. He retraced his steps and found her on the sofa, pouring a cup of tea — out of a pot no less, something he hadn't seen since he was last at his parents' house.

"I thought dips and chips, well crisps and crackers, might be just the thing after a long afternoon in the fresh air," she explained, and pointing at the second cup asked, "Milk, and or sugar?"

"Just a dash of milk please, no sugar," Dominic replied, sinking into the huge armchair. He took the proffered mug and scooped some hummus onto a rice cracker. They sat in comfortable silence for a few moments, then Dominic remarked,

"I'm not sure of the best way to phrase this, it's new to me, so I'm just going to say it. I've extended my holiday for a week. I think we're on the brink of something really special and would like to... hmmm... explore it... errr... further."

He flicked his hand between them. "If you think it's something you might be interested in doing... errr... sharing... discovering..."

He cursed his inability to articulate what he wanted to say, *way to sound like a bumbling idiot...* while distractedly running his fingers through his hair, making it even more dishevelled.

Wide-eyed, Chloe gaped at Dominic. His face was flushed, his body language, awkward — clearly, this admission did not come easily to him. Perhaps he rarely had such discussions. Something she was inordinately pleased about.

n unfamiliar glow settled around her heart. *He wanted to stay!* Maybe this was more than a cobweb dream, woven overnight only to be whisked away by an early morning breeze.

She stretched across the gap between the sofa and the chair and grasped his hand.

"I would like that very much." Her voice not much more than a whisper.

The relief washing over Dominic's face was almost comical, but all amusement fled when he stood, drew her upright and kissed her as though he never wanted to let her go.

Chloe surrendered.

The following week took on a pattern. Dominic picked up Chloe around nine, and they spent every day playing tourist.

First on the list, Castle Duart. Dating back to the thirteenth century, the castle fairly oozed history — much of it pretty gruesome — and they explored every inch. From the battlements they could see Lady's Rock, where Lady Elizabeth was abandoned to die by Sir Lachlan Mor Maclean — her ever-loving husband.

As luck would have it, she was rescued by men of her own clan, the Campbells, who were righteously upset by this heinous behaviour, and retribution was delivered by sword.

Under a blue summer sky, the rock — jutting out from the glistening Sound, against the backdrop of the mainland — looked so innocuous, it was hard to imagine such dastardly deeds were relatively commonplace.

As they descended the narrow and winding staircase, Chloe, remembering the variety of home baked cakes and scones, suggested a cuppa. Dominic was easily persuaded, and they crunched across the gravel driveway to the little tearoom adjacent to the castle.

While indulging in a slice... or two... they were surprised to see the current laird, helping himself to morning tea. He proved to be very affable, and the three chatted about Duart and Mull for a few moments. Admittedly, Chloe was a bit star-struck. To meet a clan chief was like meeting history, but she managed not to make a fool of herself.

Unfortunately, Torosay — the nineteenth century baronial castle just around the inlet from Duart — was not open to the public, but the walk through the woods from Craignure to the castle gardens, despite the latter also being closed, was worth it.

Next, they decided on a boat tour around the Treshnish Isles and Staffa, thrilled to see an abundance of wildlife, and excited at the chance to visit Fingal's Cave.

A day on Iona — known as the cradle of Christianity in Scotland — was not to be missed and they took their time. They explored the famous Abbey, and even climbed Dùn Ì, the 360-degree views from the peak, nothing short of breathtaking.

They picnicked on grassy outcrops, beside babbling streams, on rocky ledges. The weather was on their side — sunny and not too hot, with daylight lasting well into the evening.

Chloe's camera was sorely abused, she took hundreds of photos, begging Dominic to stop in the most random spots for that perfect shot of a thistle, or the scenery, or because birds of prey were soaring above them, or a herd of highland cattle just *had* to be photographed — for the thousandth time.

Dominic could not recall ever being so in tune with another person. He hated leaving her at the end of every evening and was always early to pick her up the following morning.

They talked and laughed, and the more time they spent together, the more both realised they wanted this to be more than just a holiday fling.

Despite it being obvious when they kissed — which they did *a lot* — that Dominic wanted her as much as she wanted him, Chloe was surprised and impressed he didn't take it further.

Half of her — her practical, sensible half — was relieved, it meant she didn't need to explain her lack of experience. Her other, hopelessly romantic half — yearned for him to stop being such a bloody gentleman.

Unwilling to spoil what they shared, she kept her mouth shut, unaware Dominic was fighting a similar longing.

The day before Dominic was due to leave, they returned to Calgary Beach. Chloe had expressed a desire to swim, the water around Mull more temperate than the east coast of England, near Aunt Meg's house.

Dominic, the image of Chloe stepping out of the water the first time he saw her, never far from his mind, had absolutely *no* objections, collecting her just before nine. Chloe offered to pack a picnic, but Dominic said he had it covered, so she just took her backpack, rather heavier than usual with the added weight of a couple of towels.

They returned to The Byre for coffee, taking their time, enjoying the quiet ambience of being the only customers at that time of the morning.

Soon, they were on the beach. Leaving anything valuable locked in the boot of the car, they carried only what they needed for swimming.

Chloe, who was already wearing her bikini, and had applied sunscreen before she left the cottage, shed her clothes with child-like eagerness, heading down the beach and into the sea before Dominic had removed his shirt.

"Brrrr... its cool when you first get in, but it's so beautiful, hurry up," she called to Dominic who hadn't thought to wear his trunks under his jeans, and was doing the towel shimmy to slip into them.

"Give me a sec," he yelled back and, making sure everything

was where it was supposed to be, shoved his clothes in his bag and tucked the towel in on top.

He walked down to the water's edge, standing in the gentle breakers while his feet adjusted to the cool of the sea. Chloe was waist deep, waving at him to join her. He studied her for a minute.

The crystal clear, turquoise sea enhanced her lightly tanned skin. Her hair was twisted up into a knot on the top of her head, but he could see the sun kissed highlights threading through it. Even from feet away, he discerned a mischievous glint in her glorious grey eyes, a warning she was likely thinking up ways to drench him, as soon as he got close enough.

Dominic stopped questioning, stopped over-thinking, and stopped pretending it was his imagination, or this magical isle, or simply a holiday romance.

Two things...

... he was head over heels in love with Chloe Shepherd...

... and he never wanted to leave Mull.

11

The bright sun made her squint, but nothing could have prevented Chloe from watching Dominic get changed. Through half-lidded eyes she admired the flex of his body as he shrugged out of his shirt.

Even from this distance she could tell his build was athletic but not over-muscled. She let her gaze stray, unashamedly, from his shoulders down his chest to his abs, frowning a little when he wrapped the towel around his waist. She willed it to drop — it didn't — *bugger*!

After executing the oddest wriggle, he removed the towel, shoving it and his clothes into his bag. Then, with one last check of their belongings, turned to stroll unhurriedly towards her.

Chloe gulped, she actually gulped. Even as she chastised herself for being so easily impressed, she gulped again. Had anyone asked her to describe him, she might have found enough coherence to mumble 'Greek God'.

Dominic, tall, and tanned, was wearing black swim shorts which hugged a butt you *had* to be able to bounce pennies off or, and better still, cup your hands around. Chloe, who was a regular swimmer, considered herself quite the connoisseur when it came to the male physique. She had to admit, none of the guys in the local teams held a candle to the man walking towards her with the grace and power of a panther. They were generally much slimmer, sporting broad shoulders and bulging arm muscles. To her eye, Dominic was perfectly proportioned.

Her hands itched to learn his shape, to smooth her fingers over his taut frame, and she wanted to be the only woman ever to have that privilege from now until the end of time.

Chloe stilled as the truth swirled around her like the restless waves buffeting her sun-warmed body.

She had fallen head-over-heels in love with Dominic Winters.

Meanwhile Dominic, unaware of her revelation, was pondering several things. He knew he could not stay on Mull indefinitely that wasn't an option... nice dream though.

Admitting his feelings for Chloe were far more profound than a brief fling, raised the question of what he was going to do about it. Finally, and not quite so crucial, was the plan beginning to percolate at the back of his mind.

All would have to wait; his concentration evaporated with astonishing rapidity — Chloe's body far too enticing. His lips hungered to kiss her satiny skin, chasing the droplets of water tumbling down her lithe figure. As he waded into the sea, all manner of literary descriptions along with images of Renaissance paintings popped into his head.

Good grief he *was* waxing lyrical, Kassie would be proud of him — hearing his sister's chortle of glee at her brother's complete capitulation.

He reached Chloe, who gave no indication of how affected she was by his near nakedness.

"About time," she grinned. "What took you so long? Race you, there and back." She pointed to a dark line indicating where the, much deeper, open sea met the sheltered water of the bay.

"You're on. Do you want a head start, being a girl?" he taunted, with wicked grin.

"Ha, I'd beat you, if *you* had the head start," she countered, chuckling at his expression.

"Want to bet?"

Absoflippinlutely," she put out her hand, to shake on the deal. Dominic took it and dragged her against him, kissing her soundly. "Hey, unfair tactics," she spluttered when he finally released her, her breathing going haywire.

"Whoever said I played fair?" he contested.

Chloe grumbled at him but held her peace. "Ready?"

Dominic didn't give her time to say 'go' striking out for the invisible marker.

"Oi…" Chloe shrieked, torn between berating him and falling about laughing. "You rat-bag, wait for me." She launched herself after him and the race was on.

Dominic was a reasonably strong swimmer and knew he had this in the bag. He reckoned without Chloe. He had no clue about her swimming ability. That her local pool was home to several competitive swimming squads and, for years — while managing to avoid becoming a member — Chloe had trained alongside them. It had become a regular routine. She swam for about an hour, three or four times a week. The steady rhythm was a great stress buster.

Even though Dominic was quite a way ahead of Chloe by the time she realised what he'd done, she soon caught up. Slowly, she pulled alongside, and with powerful strokes began to over-take him. She risked a glance and when she met his eye, dropped a cheeky wink, then focussed on her breathing.

There was a muffled roar, and Chloe became aware Dominic was gaining on her. The pair gave each other no quarter as they strove towards the finish line. Neither could remember where they started from, so in tacit agreement headed to the beach.

They both propelled themselves out of the waves at the same moment, water streaming off them and sprinted towards their belongings. Chloe hurled herself at the two bags, her fingers were almost touching her backpack when she felt two hands grab her ankles and yank her backwards.

"Nooooooo," she bellowed when Dominic leapt over her and touched his bag. "You rotter, that's cheating," she groused, as it seemed half the beach trickled into places she didn't want to think about.

Shuffling onto her knees, Chloe tried to brush the hot, white sand off her wet body. It was no good, she needed to dunk herself in the sea. She shot Dominic a baleful glare and stomped down to water's edge. She was mooching in the shallows trying to think up a way to get her revenge, when she heard a splash.

Without warning, Dominic grabbed her around the waist and lifted her. Before she could open her mouth, he tossed her into the slightly deeper water. Chloe rose up out of the sea like a vengeful fury, ready to clock Dominic one, only to have him take her in his arms and repeat that earth-shattering kiss.

Dominic was having more fun than he could have imagined. Chloe reminded him of Kassie and Alex — two women who although quite reticent as a general rule, became hellions when the occasion demanded.

When Chloe reared up out of the sea, water cascading off her tanned skin, Dominic once again contemplated the possibility she was a selkie, and to kiss her would prevent her slipping back to the depths — binding her to the land and him, forever.

When Chloe moulded herself to him, Dominic was all but overwhelmed by the curious sense, she was where she was supposed to be, that his life to this point was simply preparation for this moment.

A simple smile was enough to scramble his normally, very sensible, brain. Her touch could undermine him entirely. It seemed inconceivable, yet here he was kissing her as though his life depended on it.

Before his heart, not to mention parts lower, overruled his head, Dominic broke the kiss. They were both gasping for air, and Chloe's eyes were as glassy as he expected his to be.

"Have you any idea how much I want you?"

She wriggled, her wet body sliding against his. It was torture. Dominic hissed and held her still.

"I can take a wild guess," she replied, somewhat self-consciously, and he was surprised to see a blush steal over her cheeks.

"Not here," he murmured, grazing his lips over her ear.

"Where?" The word tripped over her lips before she could stop it. *Way to sound eager Chloe*, she groaned, silently.

"The cottage, later?" He made it a question, not a statement or a demand, unable, quite, to quash the plea in his voice.

He waited as Chloe leant back in his arms, her eyes searching his face. He thought his heart would either stop or explode out of his chest. After several seconds, which felt like hours, she nodded slowly, and he expelled a pent-up breath.

He held her close for a little longer, then feeling Chloe shiver, forced his mind from the delightful to the mundane. "Lunchtime I think."

I f Chloe was startled by Dominic's change of subject, she made no comment, but was pleased when he held her hand all the way back to their bags. Not discounting another swim, she just squeezed the water out of her hair, slapped on her large floppy hat, wrapped herself in one of her towels and sat on the sand, while Dominic went to get the picnic.

Her mouth fell open when she saw the size of the basket. He balanced it on a flattish rock and opened the lid.

"Good grief, how many are we feeding?" Chloe gaped at the mound of food within, enough to satisfy the hunger of a small army.

Gourmet everything from sandwiches to little pies, from the selection of miniature cakes to the carefully diced fruit. With a flourish, Dominic whipped out a blue-checked gingham cloth, making Chloe giggle.

"This reminds me of those period dramas. How very Regency or would it be Victorian?"

Dominic grinned and laid the cloth on the grass, handing out plates and glasses along with the food. "The hotel has done me proud, I never expected it to be this fancy. Not that I'm complaining." He lifted out a bottle, "even got some bubbly." He popped the cork and began pouring some into one of the glasses.

"This could be bad... I *cannot* drink at lunchtime," Chloe accepted the drink and watched the bubbles effervescing in the sunlight.

"Aww, they were kind enough to include it, we can't let it go to waste."

"On your head be it," she warned.

"How bad does it get? Dancing on tables, loud singing... ohhhh, striptease, please tell me it's a striptease," he implored, while taking the time to scan her body unhurriedly, feigning the most ludicrously lecherous expression.

Chloe burst out laughing. "Give over, you idiot. No stripping..." laughing harder when he pouted. "... there *has* been dancing, although not on tables, singing...? Hmmm... possibly... no, it's more that I fall asleep and probably snore loudly."

"Oh well, a man can hope... drink up you will need to finish most of this bottle, I'm driving."

"Mr Winters, is it your intention to get me squiffy?"

"Who me? Miss Shepherd, that's a serious accusation. I hope you have evidence to back up your claim."

Chloe waggled the glass, spilling a drop or two. "Your evidence, sir."

"You wound me," he announced over-dramatically, while offering her the platter of sandwiches. "Come on, dig in... this should soak up some of the alcohol."

They settled down to their picnic, gossiping about this and that — their jobs, lives, families and friends — the usual chitchat of people relaxed in each other's company.

As Chloe predicated, the alcohol went straight to her head. She tilted her hat until it shaded her face, leaned back against the rock, and dozed.

· · ·

Dominic contemplated Chloe while she napped. He would be leaving tomorrow, but he didn't want to go, didn't want to say goodbye. He wondered whether she felt the same way about him as he did about her. He really hoped so.

Chloe's home was about a three-hour drive from where he lived, and he knew long-distance relationships took a toll on people. His job would interfere too. He was busiest at weekends and usually only took the odd half-day here and there.

It had never bothered him before. He was a single guy, who loved his job and had plenty of friends with whom he worked. Chloe's job was Monday to Friday. Even taking into account phone calls, text messages, and traffic-free roads, the logistics were daunting.

He thought about his plan. It might just work, but he couldn't mention it to Chloe until he'd discussed it with the board, or at least one member of it. While he was sitting, he pinged a text to Alex. She'd know whether it was worthwhile broaching the subject with Jim Hazelwood, chairman of the Lanchester Hall Trust.

Her reply was immediate ~*I think that sounds like a great idea. I'll talk to Jim. When are you back and who is Chloe Shepherd? Spill, Dom!*~ accompanied by three emojis; one winking, one smiling, and one thinking.

Dominic grinned to himself, the response was typical of Alex. He sent another text, a little longer this time, receiving an ~*Ohhhhh, how exciting*~ and three hearts.

Turning off his phone, he glanced around the beach. There were a couple of people walking along the waterline, but other than that, Chloe and he were alone. Checking his watch, he noticed Chloe had been asleep for at least half an hour; it was time to wake her up.

He lifted the brim of her hat and kissed her, ever-so gently.

Chloe was lost in dreams. They featured a tall man with dark-blond hair, whose hazel eyes twinkled when he smiled. He was naked from the waist up and she was admiring his tanned body, imagining what it would be like to kiss him all the way down to where his towel hugged his hips. It was *the* most delicious fantasy.

Something shifted, wakefulness beckoned. Chloe became aware of the sun on her face and the press of lips to hers. Her eyes flickered open and her gaze collided with that same hypnotic gaze.

"Dominic...?" she whispered.

"I had to kiss you, sorry. No, I'm not sorry."

Levering herself up, Chloe responded in kind. "Why did you stop?"

"Because I was worried if I didn't, I wouldn't be able to."

Grinning at his convoluted reasoning, she teased. "I ask again, why did you stop?"

"Hey, I'm being a gentleman here."

"Well don't."

"God, Chloe." Hooking one arm around her, Dominic gathered her close and kissed her senseless. With his other hand, he unwrapped the towel, his fingers exploring every inch of her.

Encouraged, Chloe did what she craved, and scattered kisses all over his chest, her hands sliding off his shoulders, to stroke down his sides, coming to rest on his hips. Her fingers twitched at the waistband of his swimming shorts.

He groaned. "Lordy woman... uurghhhh..." when he felt her hand glide between the material and his skin, to cup then squeeze his butt.

"Chloe..." his voice was strangled, and with a Herculean effort he grabbed her wrists, dragging her hands around until they were trapped in between their bodies.

"I really don't want to end up on a charge of indecent exposure," he rasped. "Perhaps we ought to take this home?"

Chloe, inwardly gleeful at Dominic's reaction, smiled innocently. "Awww... so soon. I fancy another swim before we go."

Dominic gawked. "Errrr... swim... really? Okay." His slightly nonplussed expression at her abrupt switch in topic, comical.

"S-sorry that was t-too easy. I c-couldn't help it," Chloe stammered as she doubled over with mirth.

"Winding me up, are you? You'll pay for that, madam. What were you saying about a swim?"

In a flash he stood and, employing a fireman's lift, carried Chloe down to the water's edge, ignoring her squeals and half-hearted attempt to free herself. She tried to chastise him but couldn't for laughing.

Wading in until he was thigh deep, Dominic dropped her into the waves. He had just turned to walk out of the water, when he felt something grip his ankle. Without warning he too went under.

By the time he righted himself, Chloe was sprinting up the beach. He hauled himself out of the sea and trudged up the sand.

"Happy now?" he grumbled.

"Yes, thank you," she replied, pertly. "I got rid of any extra pesky grains of sand and dunked you. Win, win I'd say." She stood, hands on hips, grinning like a loon.

Chloe slept most of the forty-minute drive back, only rousing when Dominic pulled in behind the cottage.

"Come on sleepy head." He shook her gently. "Grab your bags and I'll bring the rest."

Chloe did as he asked and as she reached the kitchen, said she was going to take shower. "I'll only be a few minutes, then you're welcome to have one too," she added.

. . .

Dominic contemplated joining her but couldn't decide whether it was too soon. His subconscious telling him, despite his hopes for later in the evening, if he thought it was too soon — it probably was. Didn't stop his mind wandering up the stairs and into the bathroom. Maybe later...

13

True to her word, Chloe was showered in double-quick time, shouting from the top of the stairs that the bathroom was free, and she'd hung a fresh towel on the rail for him.

While she dried and dressed, the sound of the water running, conjured up an image of Dominic sponging her down. For a split second, she contemplated stripping off again and joining him — the shower was big enough for two, after all — but she held back.

Nerves, and her lack of experience making her hesitate.

Closing her mind to the tantalising thought, she went downstairs and into the kitchen where she emptied the picnic basket, putting anything perishable in the fridge and throwing out the rubbish.

Filling, and switching on the kettle, Chloe used the time it took to boil to wash the plates and glasses. She was just drying the last plate when Dominic reappeared, raking his fingers through his damp hair.

"Tea? Coffee?" she asked, "or Champagne?" Holding up the half-full bottle. "It might be a bit flat." She tilted it and peered at the liquid, then shrugged. "I can't tell, but it shouldn't go to waste."

Dominic looked at her steadily for a long moment.

"What?" she asked. "Have I missed some sand?" Rubbing at her face.

"Whether I have any more alcohol depends on one thing."

"Which is?"

"Whether you would like me to stay tonight." He watched a rosy glow bloom over Chloe's cheeks. She lowered her gaze to study the label on the bottle with fierce intensity. "Chloe?"

"I really would, it's just... well you probably... I don't..." she pressed her lips together and heaved a sigh. "I want you to stay but I haven't done this before, didn't expect... don't know how it works, well yes I know how it works... duh... it's just I've never actually, so you see..."

The words tumbled out of Chloe's mouth so fast, Dominic had trouble figuring out what she was saying. Guessing the gist, he removed the bottle from her suddenly trembling fingers, stood it on the table and stopped the torrent by dint of kissing her, soundly.

"Oh..." she said on a sigh when, eventually, he relinquished her lips. "Please do that again."

He did.

A little later they were sitting on the sofa, Chloe's legs over Dominic's, her head on his shoulder.

"I should have told you. I just didn't think you'd want to. I've never had s... hmmm... been... hmmm... intimate with anyone. How pathetic do I sound?" She bent her head, her hair falling in a silky curtain over her face hiding her embarrassment at admitting she was still a virgin at twenty-six.

Dominic tucked her hair off her face, and ran one finger along her jawline, his thumb grazing the corner of her mouth.

"Hey, it's nothing to be embarrassed about. I for one am inordinately chuffed."

She raised wary eyes to his.

Dominic took a deep breath and a leap of faith. "I am rather hoping this is going to be a forever kind of relationship, which means you'll think I'm the God of Sex." He leered at her in a very unattractive fashion.

Squashing the urge to giggle at his expression, Chloe needed a little clarification. "The forever kind?" she ventured.

"Chloe Shepherd, I love you."

She started to smile.

"Yes, it's only been a week. Yes, we barely know each other. Yes, we haven't been together long enough to call this love, blah, blah blah..."

"Blah, blah blah?"

"Technical term." He twisted on the sofa so he could cup Chloe's cheeks. Lowering his head to hers, he kissed her nose. "Anyway, before I was so rudely interrupted, I do love you, and will do so forever. I accept it's too soon to discuss marriage, but I want that too, I want it all, err... with you, in case you didn't realise..." he stopped speaking, concerned he sounded like a raving idiot.

"I love you, too." Her quiet declaration fell into the silence.

Dominic felt a grin as wide as the Sound of Mull split his face. "You do?"

She nodded. "I began falling in love with you at Eas Fors when you put your arm around my shoulders," she admitted shyly. "Then, when you told me you thought we were on the brink of something special, I realised I wanted it to be more than a holiday romance, and this afternoon, I knew for sure. Even if you hadn't felt the same, I would not have missed this week for the world."

Dominic pulled her into his arms, mildly surprised to find he actually enjoyed the feel of her hair spilling around his face.

His kiss obliterated all the others combined; a feat Chloe did not think possible.

After dinner, with which they drank the rest of the champagne, finishing off with a tot of whisky, they cleared the kitchen and put everything away. While Dominic locked the doors, Chloe leaned against the sink, abstractedly threading the tea-towel through her fingers. Her brain going into over-drive.

How did this... errr... happen? She wasn't naive enough to assume it unfolded like it did on the movies with elegance and grace, but now the moment was, presumably, here, anxiety began to gnaw at her.

What if she did it wrong? **Could** *you do it wrong? What if Dominic didn't enjoy having sex with her. Oh hell, he was going to hate having sex with her...*

Her mind was galloping like a runaway horse, and she could not prevent a whimper of panic.

Then Dominic was there, kissing her, caressing her. His fingers seeking under her T-shirt, gliding over her skin.

She shuddered, endlessly astonished at his ability to unravel her with a mere touch.

"Don't overthink it, just relax," he murmured in her ear, biting the lobe gently.

"I'm nervous."

"No, really? I would never have guessed."

Chloe felt a rumble of laugher shake his chest. "Don't laugh at me," she groused thumping him lightly on the arm. "Have you any idea how embarrassing it is not to know what to do, at my age?"

"Not a clue, but I do think the learning part will be sublime." He kissed her again, his hands roaming over her body. "Chloe." Her name a petition. "Trust me."

Somehow, they were upstairs, and in her bedroom, although Chloe never recalled how. Dominic removed her clothes with tortuous deliberation, a gesture she decided ought to be reciprocated, delighting in his response when her fingers caught his flesh.

Chloe stopped thinking, stopped worrying, almost stopped breathing, and simply let the sensations and emotions take her while Dominic wove his spell.

Clearly, this island wasn't the only possessor of magic!

14

I t was just after six the next morning when Dominic woke. He knew he should get an early start; he had a long drive ahead of him.

His original intention was to get home in one day, but as he studied Chloe, fast asleep, their bodies tangled together, he thought he might set off a bit later and have an overnight stop halfway.

Memories of the previous night caused his breathing and his heartbeat to quicken. He leaned over and pressed his lips to the soft skin at the crook of her neck, tracking along her shoulder and down her arm.

By the time he reached her elbow, Chloe was waking up. She lifted her head and stared at him, her sleepy gaze, bewildered.

"Morning," he greeted, taking advantage of her momentary confusion to shuffle her until she was on her back, exposed to him. He saw a smile curve her lips. *Holy hell, she was beautiful.*

He carried on kissing her, across her collar bone and down to the hollow between her breasts. His left hand trailed up her right leg, over her hip, coming to rest with the heel of his palm on her stomach, fingers splayed over the dip of her waist.

Chloe moaned softly, the longing in so simple a sound, like a match to dry kindling.

"Dominic..." the plea in her voice was undeniable.

He gazed down at her, bewitched by the misty hue of her eyes, darkening as her desire increased. Chloe entranced him. He didn't think he would ever get enough of her.

These thoughts were chased away when he felt her right hand snake around his waist while her left hand slid down his hip, coming around to cup him, fingers encircling him. He sucked in a sharp breath.

"I love you, Chloe..." he captured her mouth with his, the inevitable heat blazing through them.

To be woken by a kiss is every girl's dream, thought Chloe drowsily, climbing through layers of sleep opening her eyes to see Dominic's head and feel his lips along her arm.

Her brain was sluggish and not as fast as her eyes. *There's a man in my bed. Am I still dreaming?* Her head caught up, scenes from last night tumbling though her mind.

She raised herself slightly as Dominic turned and spoke to her, his words coming from a distance. He moved her until she was lying on her back. She felt she ought to cover herself up but the hunger in his beautiful eyes transfixed her. *Could you call men's eyes, beautiful? Hell yes!*

She smiled up at him, then lost the ability to concentrate as his lips scorched a path over her already sensitive skin, unable to stop herself from arching into him.

"Dominic..." she couldn't think of what to say, how to entreat him to make love to her again and again, without actually begging — although at this point, she was more than happy to beg.

Common sense dictated she let her body rest, but common sense be damned. Dominic was leaving — she could rest after he had gone. Her whole being craved his touch. She hooked one hand around his waist, while her other ventured lower, a wicked grin twitching at her mouth when she heard him hiss. She wriggled against him, hearing his breathing hitch.

"I love you, Chloe." The emotion in his voice reverberated through her, as he staked his claim with a fiery kiss — a claim to which she surrendered without the slightest protest.

———

Hours later than planned, Dominic said goodbye. He still had to pack his belongings, check out of his room at the hotel and catch the Oban ferry.

Chloe pinned a smile on her face and waved madly as he drove away. Her heart ached, and tears burned behind her eyes, but she refused to let him see; he needed all his wits for the drive. They already had each other's phone numbers, to this they added email and home addresses.

"Maybe you could come stay with me on your way home?" Dominic had suggested while they ate a very late breakfast.

"You sure?" Now it was time for him to leave, Chloe was pestered by the unsettling notion she would never see him again.

"Chloe, what I said last night." He waited until he saw her nod. "I meant every word. I want to marry you, I want to spend the rest of my life with you, but I also want to do the old-fashioned thing and date you... no, I prefer court you... before I propose. Not saying it will be a long courtship. I'm thinking two months tops."

He waggled his eyebrows, making her laugh. "Also, please think about my idea, the one about you creating note cards and postcards, fridge magnets and letter heads with your beautiful photographs. I know they will be very popular."

He stood up from his chair and drew her close. "I love you so much, it's doing my head in that I have to go." Cupping her nape, he entwined his fingers into her glossy hair, and rested his forehead to hers. Then he kissed her slowly, tenderly, leisurely.

Now he was gone. Pushing herself off the door jamb, Chloe went back into the cottage. She tidied up the kitchen, washed and dried the crockery. Trudging upstairs, she surveyed the disaster area that was her bedroom. Clothes and bedding strewn about haphazardly.

Fighting an urge to have a good old tantrum, then give in to a bout of sobs, she pulled herself together and sorted out the mess.

After downing two coffees, strong enough to dissolve a spoon, Chloe decided to drive along Loch Na Keal and maybe onto Bunessan. It was another stunning day, not to be wasted just because she was sad.

Dominic texted and called with gratifying regularity. Their last chat of the day was when they were both in bed, his topic of conversation leaving her in no doubt what he wished he was doing instead of spending the night alone in a B & B, not far from Edinburgh.

The frequent contact made Chloe feel close to Dominic, despite the miles separating them.

15

Chloe, with nearly two weeks left of her holiday, pondered Dominic's suggestion. It was a subject which began to fill her evenings. A blessing, since she was unexpectedly lonely. An emotion she rarely experienced prior to meeting Dominic. She had always relished being on her own, to read, or watch a movie, never needing company.

Aunt Meg was often out in the evenings, she had a multitude of societies and clubs she belonged to and, after a long day at the office, Chloe was thankful for a few hours without having to talk. After Dominic left, she found the time between dinner and bed hung heavily, and his idea proved to be a riveting diversion.

She researched the pros and cons of setting up your own business; the legal and technical requirements, the costs, and whether she was going to be a tiny fish in a vast ocean, with little chance of making enough money to live off the proceeds.

Regardless of the possible pitfalls, Chloe discovered she really wanted to give it a go. One afternoon, five days after Dominic's departure, she called Aunt Meg and discussed it with her.

"I think it could be wonderful for you," her aunt's voice floated tinnily through the phone. "You hate your job and this way you can travel for work. It won't be easy, but you're young enough to take the risk. If it doesn't work, at least you've tried, and I have no doubt you'll regret it if you don't."

"That was my thought too, Aunt Meg. I'm really excited about the prospect of doing something I love. Dominic said—"

"Dominic?" Aunt Meg's tone rose on a question.

"Yeah, you know, Dominic Winters, the guy I was telling you about."

The line went quiet.

"Aunt Meg? Are you still there?"

"How much do you know about this Dominic?"

"More than I am going to share with you."

Another silence.

"Chloe?"

"Yes."

"Have you slept with him?"

"Aunt Meg!" Chloe gasped, momentarily robbed of breath. "Really?"

Well, have you?"

"Whether I have or not is my business and nothing to do with this conversation. Aunt Meg, I'm twenty-six, please."

"Just looking out for you, poppet." Meg reverted to Chloe's pet name, one she hadn't used for years.

"And I love you for it, but this is all very new to me, and I'm not ready to talk about it."

"Promise me you won't rush into anything,

Too late, thought Chloe, closing her eyes briefly, Dominic's face danced behind her eyelids. "I promise."

They chatted some more, then Chloe disconnected and dialled Dominic's number.

"Hey beautiful," his voice sent shivers all the way through her. "How's my favourite girl?"

74

"I'm okay, you?"

"All good. How can I help you?" Her call unusual in the middle of the afternoon.

"I've been talking to my Aunt Meg about your idea. I think I want to give it a go, but not as a side line. I want to quit my job and concentrate on building up a small business." She waited to hear his thoughts.

Dominic and she had already discussed the details, but until now, Chloe had been reluctant to let go of her stable job, however boring it was. The income would be helpful until she knew whether this would be a successful venture.

"I think that sounds great." Dominic sounded almost as enthusiastic as she was. He paused for a second, then continued.

"Chloe, I've been talking to Alex. We have been thinking of putting together several brochures and a coffee table book about the Hall. The brochures to be handed out with the tickets, would be seasonal, spotlighting the different courses and crafts available at any given time. The coffee table book would showcase Lanchester Hall as a whole and be sold in the gift shop.

"Alex and the board would like to see a portfolio of your work with a view to commissioning you to take the requisite photographs. As it will be a year in the life of the estate, you would need to be prepared to work here for at least that period."

Chloe could scarcely believe her ears. "I-I'm s-sorry, w-what now?" she croaked.

Dominic repeated himself, amusement clear in his voice. He could just imagine Chloe's expression. "It's not a given, but I've seen your photographs, I know you have the talent and the eye to produce what the board is looking for."

"How soon would they need it?"

"If you think you could bring it with you when you stop here on your way home, that'd be perfect. It also means you *have* to stay with me."

"How many photos and of what would they want, do you know?"

"Just a broad selection — animals, scenery, plants, flowers, birds... just promise me you'll include that highland cow and calf you took, the day after we met."

"Okay," she replied, a little diffidently, feeling heat creep up her cheeks.

"Why are you blushing?"

"How on earth could you know that?"

"I can tell by your voice."

"Dominic..." she hesitated.

"Yes, love."

"Do you really think I can do this?" Her voice dropped to a whisper

"Absoflippinlutely." His reply reminded her of the day on Calgary Beach.

She sucked in a breath. "Okies, I'm on it. Operation Portfolio has begun. I have to go, talk to you later, love you." She hung up before Dominic had chance to say another word.

Chuckling, he placed his phone on the desk next to him — Chloe's face smiling up at him from his lock screen — and got back to work.

Chloe researched printing places on Mull and discovered there was a service available at the Hebridean Lodge in Tobermory. Not only a printing place but, apparently, there was also a shop and a restaurant in the sane complex. Score!

She spent the rest of the day browsing through her photos, already uploaded onto her laptop, selecting thirty. Approximately a third were of Mull, a third were images of several places across Yorkshire, and a third were a variety of flora and fauna taken during different seasons. Chloe copied them onto a thumb drive ready for the morning.

Satisfied with her efforts, she treated herself to dinner at the Italian restaurant not far from the cottage.

The following day she drove into Tobermory and spent an hour or so discussing what she wanted with the printer, who confirmed the pictures would be ready the next afternoon.

It wasn't a cheap exercise, but Chloe reasoned it was worth the expense. It would only have to be done once, adding or removing photographs from time to time, to update the collection.

She found a lovely art folio in the stationary shop and, after hunting around, spotted a pack of blank business cards with a C, fashioned after an illuminated letter, in one corner. They would do until she decided upon a proper logo. She also hunted down a calligraphy pen and small bottle of dark purple ink with which to write her name on the card.

Pleased with her purchases, Chloe took the long way home, stopping for lunch at The Byre, where she enjoyed another bowl of Crofter's Soup, and bought Aunt Meg the beautiful wool scarf she'd spotted the day she and Dominic came for lunch that first time.

Back at the cottage, she played around with names, finally deciding on the simple but, she believed, easily remembered — *Photos by Chloe*. She practised writing this with the calligraphy pen, eventually risking a test on one of the cards. It was a reasonable effort, but it wasn't quite right, and it took several more attempts before she was happy.

Shoulders and neck aching from bending over the table for so long, Chloe stretched, aware her phone was pinging. Three missed calls from Dominic and two texts. Goodness she hadn't heard the normally invasive trill. It was nearly 7pm. Wow, it was only just after two when she got home — time really did fly when you were enjoying yourself.

She rang Dominic and apologised, making him laugh when she told him why she missed his call.

"I hope it will look professional enough. I haven't got time to come up with a business name or a logo. I'll do all that when I get home. "

"Stop panicking, it will be fine," Dominic reassured, then diverted her with a far more interesting topic of conversation — what he had planned when she stayed with him.

16

———

Chloe was back at the printers just after midday and declared herself delighted with the result. The printer had suggested several different styles and sizes of print making the portfolio more interesting.

He had even included a couple that looked as though the image was taken through a large three-paned, picture window. Chloe was ecstatic, the cost nothing compared with how professional they looked.

"Thank you so much, I am eternally grateful you were able to fit my order in at such short notice."

"My pleasure, Miss Shepherd. I look forward to seeing more of your work."

"You are too kind." She smiled and said her goodbyes. Once home, she took a few photos, texting them to Dominic, before calling and nearly deafening him when she squealed her excitement.

"Dominic, did you get my texts? Don't the pictures look amazing? The printer has done me proud."

She rattled on for a few minutes, until Dominic interjected.

"They look incredible. Sorry, I can't chat, I'm on my way to a meeting. I'll call you later." He sounded terse, and his tone put Chloe on her guard.

"Dammit, sorry I never thought, I was just so chuffed."

"Never apologise for being happy, Chloe. I wish I had time, but I haven't. Love you."

She had no chance to reply. He'd hung up.

Ugh, what an idiot, Chloe plonked herself down at the kitchen table. Dominic's hint of impatience stirred up unpleasant memories, and she heard her parents' admonishments in her head. 'No one's interested, Chloe, go upstairs and play,' or 'Don't interrupt dear, the adults are talking,' or 'calm down, Chloe you are always so... excitable,' ...when they bothered to acknowledge her existence at all.

She drew a breath. It wasn't rational or fair to align Dominic with her parents. Of course, he was busy, she just hadn't given it a thought when she rang. *Mind he could have turned his phone off. Her call would have gone to message bank, saving her from interrupting his oh so important day*, a disgruntled voice at the back of her head goaded.

This whole falling in love thing was a bloody minefield. She knew they would not always agree. The odd argument or misunderstanding was inevitable. Chloe rested her head in her hands and took stock.

He was the one who extended his holiday, on nothing more than a whim really. *He* was the one who suggested her for this commission. Two of the, probably many, things he had no need to do *if* he was lying to her about his feelings. Neither of which were quite enough to quell the voices whispering that she was out of sight out of mind.

·   ·   ·

I need to get out. Tidying the photos, Chloe stored them safely in her bedroom. Then she grabbed her backpack and car keys. It was quite late, so she just drove along Loch Na Keal to Eas Fors.

Parking in the lay-by, she went for a walk. Needing to breathe in the familiar air, and hear the babbling chatter of the waterfall. The weather was miserable, heavy clouds hung over the island. She couldn't see the peak of Ben More. She could barely see the islands in the loch.

It suited her mood. She had been so happy to get the pictures and now she was questioning the whole thing. Then her common sense kicked in. Chloe was pretty sure Dominic was not the kind of man to say he loved you and not mean it... *was he*? What did she really know about him? Everything he told her could have been a pack of lies. Well, there was one way to find out.

Sitting on a rocky outcrop overlooking the loch, Chloe unlocked her phone and prayed for a signal, smiling when she saw two bars at the top. She searched for Alex Faulkner and Lanchester Hall. There was a decent amount of information.

Apparently, the house had become a Trust relatively recently and was currently in the process of introducing a number of courses to teach the multitude of traditional skills and crafts required on old estates. It was fascinating stuff. In her mind's eye, she could already envisage how the photographs would be composed.

Searching the website, she eventually found the section featuring the staff, inordinately relieved when she spotted Dominic listed as Estate Steward. Reading his bio, Chloe was glad to note it gelled with what he told her.

She felt a bit mean, doubting his word, yet savvy enough to know how easy it was to take someone at face value only to discover they were not who they purported to be. Accepting that by proving it to herself now was a bit like closing the gate after the horse has bolted, Chloe's disquiet was allayed.

Before dropping her phone in her bag, she twisted on the rock, snapped a selfie with Ulva and the murky-grey of the loch in the background. She pinged it to Dominic with the message ~*Sorry I interrupted you earlier. Wish you were here!*~ and added the blowing kisses emoji.

Chloe didn't wait for it to send. It could take ages with it having the photo attachment. She sat for a little longer, but the rain was getting heavier, and a mist was descending. It was time to go home.

She glanced at her watch. It was coming up to half five. Deciding scrambled eggs on toast with a glass of wine sounded just right for dinner, she sauntered back to the car.

Switching on Bessie's headlights, Chloe checked to make sure there was no oncoming traffic and eased out. She debated whether she needed fog-lights too, deciding it wasn't necessary. She could see the road well ahead of her. Chloe drove carefully. This road was dicey enough in fine weather with excellent visibility, it was ten times worse in the rain.

A couple of miles from the head of the loch, she came to a rise, after which the road dropped away quite steeply, curving to the right in the hollow. Familiar with this particular section, Chloe decelerated further to negotiate it.

She was almost at the bottom of the bank, when a car shot around the bend, coming straight at her, far too fast for the conditions, its headlights, on full-beam, temporarily blinding her.

The road wasn't wide enough to allow them to pass. The oncoming driver made no allowances for other road users and the car slewed towards her on the slick tarmac.

Chloe heard the blare of a horn. *Stupid idiot, how the hell was she supposed to get out of his way? He was the one driving like a bloody maniac.* She had nowhere to go and a split second to get there... *Shit!*

The only way to avoid a collision with the other car was to drive off the road.

Chloe stomped on the brakes and yanked her steering wheel sharply to the left. The wheels bumped over the soft gravel and rocks strewn at the roadside. Despite her slow speed, the car bounced onto the verge, then tipped forward.

There was a crunch of metal and, in slow motion, her car slid inelegantly into a ditch.

17

Shock rendered Chloe motionless, and she gripped the steering wheel as though it was a lifeline, praying the culvert wasn't deep. The car sank a little then settled at an awkward angle.

Heart pounding, Chloe tried to open the door, but it was wedged against the side of the ditch. *Awesome.* The wipers swished across the windshield, which was intact. Peering through she spotted lights a little way up the slope of the hill in front of her.

With trembling fingers, Chloe switched off the engine, unclipped her seatbelt and inched across to the passenger side. It was no good, the door must have buckled because it refused to open. Chloe slapped her palm on the wheel, furious with the asshat who had caused this accident and driven off without a care.

The ramifications of a damaged car began to spin around her head. A head, Chloe realised, was aching. *Had she banged it?* *Bloody hell, this was all she needed.* Her return home would doubtless be delayed. She couldn't afford to hire a car for that distance — it being one-way adding to the expense — as well as pay for repairs. Any delay might also mean forfeiting the possible commission from Lanchester Hall.

First things first. She couldn't stay here all night. Shuffling back to the driver's seat, Chloe turned on the ignition just enough for the electrics to work. She pressed the button at the top of the arm rest. As the window slid down, she was pelted by rain. Nope, that wouldn't work.

Closing the window, Chloe pondered her options. If she climbed out this way, the interior of the car would get soaked because she had no way of shutting the window from the outside.

Twisting, she stared around the back of the car. Doubtless, there was a clever way to open the boot from inside, but she had no clue how, and suspected it involved removing half the plastic trim. The left side, rear passenger window was her best option. The slant of the car would prevent the rain from blowing in, and also meant it was unlikely anyone else would notice the open window.

Decision made, Chloe scrabbled about in the passenger footwell for her bag, which had shot off the seat when she slammed on the brakes. Double checking she had everything in it, especially her phone and keys, Chloe hooked it securely over her shoulder, and wriggled through the gap between the seats.

Winding down the rear window, she inched her way out gingerly. Her arm muscles — strengthened from all that swimming — held her in good stead. It took some time, because the sides of the ditch were muddy and slippery but, eventually, Chloe managed to manoeuvre herself out of the car and out of the ditch.

Heaving a sigh of relief, she stood on shaky legs and surveyed the damage. It wasn't good, but she was no expert, maybe it was salvageable. Nothing she could do about it right now.

Surveying her surrounds, Chloe saw the lights were indeed from what looked like a house. She walked along the road for a few yards until she came to the driveway and headed up the gentle incline to the front door.

She rapped the knocker. The door was opened by a young woman who assessed her unexpected visitor's bedraggled appearance in a heartbeat, and ushered inside the now drenched Chloe.

"What happened, lass?" The soft Scottish burr along with the cosy ambience of the kitchen went a long way to soothing Chloe's fright.

Chloe explained and asked her hostess whether she knew the number for a towing company.

"Och, lass, dinna wirra about that, Sam'll get it out for you in the morning. Canna do anything about it tonight. Are ye hurt?"

"I don't think so, and are you sure, I don't want to inconvenience... Sam did you say his name was?"

"Ay, and he'll no' mind. Sit yerself there and I'll get you a towel. I'm Ainsley McEwan, by the way, sorry to meet you in such horrible circumstances."

"You are so kind, Ainsley, thank you. I'm very pleased to meet you, I'm Chloe Shepherd."

Chloe's teeth were starting to chatter, her lips were turning a lovely shade of blue and she was shivering — although she hadn't noticed.

Ainsley hurried out of the kitchen returning seconds later with a huge fluffy towel, in which she bundled Chloe. "Sam'll be home in a wee bit. I'll make us a nice cuppa while we wait. Where are you staying?"

"Salen, in one of the cottages."

The two women gossiped over a hot mug of tea and a dram of whisky each. Ainsley insisted, saying it was positively the quickest way to get warm. Chloe wasn't complaining, she was feeling wretched.

Half an hour slipped by, and Chloe was starting to warm up. Ainsley was topping up their mugs with fresh tea, when the door burst open bringing in a flurry of cold air, and a giant of a man, who ducked his head to avoid banging it on the lintel. Ainsley introduced the two to each going on to explain what had happened.

"Ay, I just saw the wreck. You okay, lass? You're no' hurt?" The aforementioned Sam said, solicitously.

"Thank you, I don't think so, although my head aches a bit. I 'spect that's just shock."

Sam scanned her pale face, spying a faint bruise forming above her eyebrows. "I think you might have banged your forehead, but it doesn't look too bad."

"I was only going about ten miles an hour. It was just the wet road and I ended up in the ditch. All I can say is I'm glad it was there, not further back. I might have ended up in the loch, and from much higher up." If possible, Chloe's face went whiter still. The thought of what might have been, made her stomach roil.

"Come on, lass, let's get you home. An early night for you, I reckon."

Chloe smiled her gratitude and unwrapped herself from the towel, folding it neatly. She repeated her thanks to Ainsley, who gave her a hug, before following Sam out to his big four-wheel drive.

"Should I put some kind of warning about my car?" she queried as she buckled in.

"I've placed a couple of reflective triangles on the approach, that ought to do the trick." Sam reassured.

Chloe relaxed against the comfortable leather of the car seat and, when they reached Salen, directed Sam to her cottage.

He helped her out and unlocked the door for her, frowning a little at how cold she seemed. "Sure you'll be all right?" he asked when she thanked him for the third time.

"I'll be fine. I'll have a hot shower, and some soup and probably another whisky. Then I'll go to bed." She shook his hand. They swapped mobile numbers and he confirmed he would let her know to which garage he towed the car.

"I do appreciate everything you've done for me. I cannot thank you and your wife enough." Chloe reiterated.

"It's nothing, lass. Can't leave you stranded. I'm just glad it wasn't worse. I'll be in touch." He waved and was gone.

Chloe locked up and, after switching on the kettle, went upstairs for a long hot shower. Dried and dressed, her wet attire in the laundry sink, Chloe felt almost human again. She had something to eat and, wrapping herself in a fleecy blanket, curled up on the sofa with a hot chocolate and a whisky chaser.

This was the first moment she had thought to check her phone. Two voicemails and three texts, all from Dominic. The basic gist of all five were 'where was she?' Although the last text was rather brusque.

She supposed she ought to feel pleased he cared enough to be frustrated when he didn't get a reply. Whisky cradled in one hand, Chloe rang Dominic's number and waited.

18

___

Dominic answered on the first ring. "Chloe, why have been ignoring my calls and texts? You been caught up with your photos again?" His tone a blend of relief, amusement, and irritation.

"This is the first chance I've had. There was no signal this afternoon, and I wasn't ignoring you. I had a bit of an accident."

"What do you mean 'a bit of an accident'?"

"I came off the road not far from the falls."

"Shit, Chloe, I said you have to pay attention along that road. Were you going too fast for the conditions?" Dominic added a tactless remark about careless drivers.

His remarks sent a wave of anger through Chloe who was already overly emotional.

"You're kidding me, right? Why would you assume *I* was the one in the wrong? Because I'm a woman? *I'm* not the one who drives like a bat out of hell. I *was* concentrating, it was the other idiot driving too fast around a blind bend, forcing me off the road who wasn't concentrating. He didn't stop to check on me, by the way, he just carried on, leaving me stuck in a ditch. Thankfully, apart from a bump on my head, I'm fine, thanks for asking," she hissed.

"I work for an insurance assessor, Dominic. I've seen first-hand what happens when you take risks behind the wheel. Do you really think I would not take care, driving on these roads? How *dare* you accuse me of incompetence. *Bite me!*"

Chloe sucked in a breath, knowing when she got aggravated, she tended to lose intelligibility.

"So, now I have no car and no idea when the repairs, if indeed it is repairable, will be complete. My departure will be delayed indefinitely because I cannot afford to pay for repairs *and* hire a car, and I have too much stuff to travel home on public transport, but hey... don't you worry about that.

"This means it's unlikely I'll be able to keep my appointment at Lanchester Hall. Perhaps that's for the best, I certainly don't want them to think badly of you for recommending someone who is so obviously incapable of mastering the most basic tasks, like driving a car properly," she blurted out, vaguely aware she was not making a whole lot of sense.

"I'll email them and let them know, with my apologies. This whole thing was clearly a mistake. A deliriously beautiful, tantalisingly, glorious mistake, but a mistake all the same. Thank you for a fantastic week."

She hit the red disconnect icon, without saying goodbye, wishing they had been talking on an actual land line so she could slam down the receiver. Cutting the call on a tiny and silent red disk did not have the same dramatic effect.

Her phone rang immediately but she ignored it, and then turned it off. Yes, she was being petty, and had overreacted, but Dominic's curious attitude earlier and immediate assumption she was in the wrong, pushed all her buttons, rousing her innate lack of self-confidence.

She swallowed the last of her whisky and, uncaring it was only half eight, went to bed.

Sitting on the sofa in his apartment on the Lanchester estate, Dominic gaped at his phone. *How in the **hell** had that escalated to what sounded like a break-up?* He ran his mind over their conversation. Well, it wasn't really a conversation. He'd barely had the chance to speak, before she started railing at him.

Then he recalled what he *had* said and, groaning, palmed his forehead. He redialled Chloe's number, but it went straight to voicemail. He swore, *a lot*, then sent an email and a text, apologising for being a dickhead, begging her to call him as soon as she got his message.

He spent a sleepless night, worrying whether he'd just blown the best thing ever to happen to him.

Chloe woke at first light the next morning, the soft golden glow of dawn heralding a sunny day. She ached all over — no surprise there. Dragging herself out of bed, she stood under the hot jets of the shower and let the water pummel her body.

While drying her hair, she inspected her face, noting the darkening bruise on her forehead, still unable to recall banging it. Chloe grimaced at her appearance, and then shrugged. She couldn't change it. Dominic had seemed to like her just as she was.

Dominic. Images of their week together flickered through her head. She owed him an apology. She had woken several times during the night, her angry response to his insinuation that the accident was her fault, playing on her mind. He had no right to assume anything, but she didn't give him chance to retract his words. Chloe was honest enough to admit she was partially to blame for her restless night.

While her tea brewed, she switched on her phone and heard several pings. Before checking her messages, she rang Aunt Meg and told her what happened.

As expected, her aunt was concerned, but knew Chloe was quite able to handle most things. Not convinced Chloe's subdued tone was solely related to the accident, Meg made a mental note to call her niece again the next day.

About to hang up, Chloe added, "I'm going to put in my notice today. I love the guys I work for, but I can't go back to that job, now something far more interesting seems possible. If I'm not reckless, I think I have enough savings to keep me afloat for a couple of months. I might have to pay for the repairs up front, but even if I do, the insurance ought to cover all costs except the excess, which isn't too steep."

"Good for you, dear. Now are you sure you are not injured, you don't have concussion or hidden internal injuries?"

"I'm fine, Aunt Meg, truly. I could walk faster than the car was going, and if the ditch hadn't been there, I wouldn't be in this predicament. Unfortunately, it was, and Bessie is a bit crumpled."

Chloe didn't mention the bruise on her head. What Aunt Meg didn't know couldn't worry her. They chatted a few more moments, then Chloe said her goodbyes and promised to keep her aunt updated.

Her second call was to the office. Her boss, Phil, was sorry to hear she was resigning, but understood she wanted a change. She had worked for Phil long enough not to prevaricate, telling him about the accident and the likely delay it might cause, along with what she hoped to be doing.

Phil said he would ask the temp whether she wanted to stay on permanently and if so, Chloe didn't have to work her notice. She had been a reliable employee and rarely took her full allotment of holidays, therefore, he was happy to class this last month as her notice period. He would let her know what the temp said, and on that note, they ended their conversation.

Once that was sorted, Chloe accessed her messages. One was from Sam. He'd hauled the car out of the ditch and taken it to the garage in Salen. They would be able to provide her with more information after they'd assessed it.

She rang Sam to let him know she'd got his message, thanking him again for all his help.

Finally, she read the message from Dominic, her mouth curving in amusement at his words. *~Chloe, I'm sorry. I was a total arsehole, whom you should never speak to again for being such an insensitive git, but I hope you will because I do love you, and hope I haven't screwed everything up~*

She found his name in her recent list and called him.

19

"Chloe, I'm an idiot, forgive me?" Were Dominic's first words when he answered, almost before it started to ring.

"Only if you forgive me too," Chloe beseeched, contritely.

"What the hell do I need to forgive you for?" Dominic sounded startled

"I overreacted. I wasn't at my best and I kinda got the impression you were irritated with me when I rang earlier, so I just lashed out. It's like a coping mechanism, I guess... stop it before it can hurt me, type of thing."

"I would never intentionally hurt you, Chloe. I didn't mean to be abrupt when you rang, my head was full of the agenda for the meeting, and I wasn't concentrating. Later, when I hadn't heard from you, I started to worry. No, to be honest, I was panicking. You normally reply almost immediately, ten minutes or so, max, nearly five hours and I was climbing the walls. Then you tell me you'd had an accident and I didn't think."

His self-deprecating tone made Chloe smile.

"After you hung up on me, and I'd finished kicking myself, I got your text with the photo, and wanted to kick myself all over again." Humour crept into his voice.

"Ok, how about we accept we both behaved like brats, and move on?" Chloe suggested.

"I like your thinking. Wait, please tell me you haven't cancelled your appointment with Jim Hazelwood?"

"No, I haven't had chance. I probably wouldn't have done, it's too good an opportunity. Like I say, I was just venting."

"Phew, good to hear. I transferred the images you sent onto my desktop, the printer you found did an awesome job, they are stunning. I sent a couple on to Alex, and she agrees with me."

"I spent a bit of time on the Lanchester Hall website. I already have loads of ideas, the place is a photographer's dream, and with all those workshops... I can't wait to start. If I'm approved, of course," she added, awkwardly.

"I suspect it's only a formality," Dominic said, not at liberty to inform Chloe, the board had sanctioned his recommendation, subject to seeing her portfolio.

"Well, I've still got a few days left here, maybe my car is repairable. I'll have to see about hiring a bike or something, I don't want to be stuck at the cottage for a week. Anyway, enough about me, what have you been up to, other than being rude about your girlfriend's driving."

Chloe bit her lip and rolled her eyes at her runaway tongue; thankful Dominic was miles away. In spite of everything, assuming she was Dominic's girlfriend — a term which sounded ridiculously juvenile when you were twenty-six — seemed... presumptuous.

"Dammit, that just slipped out," she muttered.

She heard a chuckle.

"I rather like hearing you refer to your self as my girlfriend, makes me feel young again."

"Young? You're not old, anyone'd think you were eighty-six not thirty-six," Chloe admonished with a grin.

"Will you love me when I'm eighty-six?"

"Fishing, Dominic? Hmm... that will depend on whether you trust me behind the wheel and will let me drive," she teased.

In his quiet office, Dominic Winters smiled at the phone screen. "I promise I trust you and am happy to let you drive."

"In that case, I promise I will love you when you are eighty-six, possibly even as old as ninety-six. After that, I'll probably trade you in for a younger model," she tossed out airily, and he heard her gurgle of laughter.

God, he missed her.

Much as it would have fun to chat all morning, Dominic had to hang up, work awaited. A thought crossed his mind, he let it roll around while he waded through a pile of documents, requiring his signature.

He was pushing his luck but, because of his years of service, before and after Lanchester Hall became a Trust, there was an unspoken rule. As long as he was up to date with nothing vital pending, he could take holidays to suit himself. His team was reliable and efficient, they wouldn't cock anything up.

Decision made, Dominic sent an email to Jim, copying in Alex, explaining why he would appreciate being granted another week's leave, even though he had just returned to work. The circumstances were... unusual and he played on their desire to begin work on the brochures, as soon as possible. Plus, he really wanted to see Chloe. He could never have imagined three weeks ago, missing someone as much as he missed her.

With nothing to do but wait, Dominic pushed everything else to the back of his mind and applied himself to his job.

Chloe sauntered around to the garage where Sam had taken her car. She introduced herself and after discussing the damage to Bessie, asked whether they knew of anywhere she could hire a bike or even a small car.

The owner of the garage, a Mr Buchanan, said they had a hatchback he loaned out on occasion and, since she knew Sam, he would give her a good deal.

If Mr Buchanan thought she was a friend of Sam's, Chloe wasn't about to contradict him, thanking the genial owner with a relieved smile.

She completed the paperwork and shortly thereafter was driving off the forecourt in a smart little Mazda.

The next couple of days flew by. Mr Buchanan confirmed Bessie was repairable, it would probably take about two weeks, because they needed to order parts.

Chloe wasn't fazed. She had resigned from her job and, after speaking to the agent managing the cottage, discovered the next booking was the one Dominic had mentioned the day after they met — a month away. Chloe extended two more weeks and prayed her car would be fixed by then.

She took a bouquet, and a bottle of whisky to the McEwans in gratitude for their kindness. The couple welcomed Chloe as though they had known her for years, and by the end of the afternoon, a new friendship was cemented.

All in all, life was good. She missed Dominic, but they talked two or three times a day, and she knew she'd be seeing him soon.

Unbeknownst to Chloe, Dominic was about to surprise her. His week's leave was approved as he guessed it would be. Alex merely commented that she couldn't wait to meet the woman who had him dashing into the wilds of Scotland at the drop of a hat.

Not quite a week after Chloe's car accident, Dominic boarded the ferry at Lochaline. It was a perfect summer's day. The sun shone down from a cloudless blue sky. Mull drifted on a sparkling sea; the only thing marring the tranquil waters of the Sound was the wake from the ferry.

Dominic inhaled a long deep breath. He loved his work, his life at Lanchester Hall and being close to family, but Mull, even though his visits were infrequent, always felt like home.

Disembarking at Fishnish, he drove the short distance to Salen, not expecting to find Chloe at the cottage but wanting to check anyway. He spent a few moments pondering her whereabouts, then gave her a quick call.

She picked up after three rings.

"Dominic," she greeted him, cheerfully. "How are you? I was just thinking about you."

"Should I be flattered?" He heard a chuckle.

"I've just parked at the pull-in where we first met. Thankfully, there are no lambs stuck in bogs, so I am at least clean. I might go for a swim though; it's beautiful here today, hot and sunny. How is it with you?"

"A bit cloudy but nice enough," he prevaricated. They chatted for a few minutes, then Dominic ended the call saying he'd ring her again when he finished work.

Seconds later he heard the ping of a text message. Checking it, he grinned, Chloe had sent a photo of her foot as proof she was paddling.

Using his spare key, he dumped his bags inside the cottage, locked up, and pointed the car towards Gribun.

20

The route to the pull-in seemed to take twice as long as usual but, eventually, Dominic spotted what he guessed was her hire car, a small Mazda, and parked alongside it. No sign of Chloe.

Securing his car, he strolled down to the water's edge. As he gazed across to Inch Kenneth, movement caught his eye. A seal was bobbing just beyond the shallows. Grabbing his phone, he swiped to access the camera. As he did so, the seal stood up.

It was like déjà vu — only this time Dominic recognised the vision walking towards him. Chloe was wearing a patterned, bright turquoise, one-piece; the swimming costume, accentuating her svelte curves and complementing her tan.

He felt his body pulse in response, *get a grip Dominic, you're worse than a sex-starved teenager*. He knew the instant Chloe spotted him.

She paused, and he could almost hear her brain ticking over. Then she increased her pace, splashing through the gently undulating waves.

"Dominic?" Her startled question carried in the still air. "*Dominic?*" Disbelief clear in her voice.

He met her on the narrow stretch of sand between the loch and the grassy bank, uncaring that he was fully clothed, and she was saturated.

"Chloe..." he gathered her into his arms and kissed her cold mouth and her damp eyelids and her wet cheeks, his fingers entangling into her dripping hair.

"How... when... did... what?" Chloe stammered when she was allowed to take a breath.

"Later," he replied and kissed her again.

Chloe had been swimming only a matter of minutes when she heard the crunch of tyres on the gravel of the pull-in. She groaned inwardly, it was so lovely having the place to herself. She couldn't fault any tourist for stopping — the view from here was magnificent — but she was enjoying the peace. She swam a little longer, then feeling the sand under her fingers on her downstroke, stood, to walk the last few yards.

A man was facing her, holding his phone in a manner suggesting he had been taking photos. Frowning, Chloe felt she ought to tick him off when she blinked, stared and blinked again. It couldn't be. She was just talking to him, and he said it was cloudy in Northumberland.

"Dominic?"

Was she imagining things?

She repeated his name and he moved towards her.

It *was* him. *How in the hell?*

She didn't care how he got there, the fact remained, he *was* there. Right in front of her. She splashed towards him as fast as she could go, squeaking with surprise when he took no notice of her sodden state and wrapped his arms around her. His lips descended on hers with barely suppressed passion.

She tried to ask how he was there, when he was just at work. He ignored her questions and carried on kissing her.

Reluctantly, Dominic released her. Both of them wanted so much more.

Chloe shook her head, still stunned by his presence.

"I can't believe you're here. Why? How? Not that I'm complaining by the way."

"I missed you and, after our... *my*... thoughtless reaction, realised I had to apologise in person.

"That wasn't necessary, but I'm very glad you thought it was." Chloe dusted light kisses along his jaw up to his ear, gently nipping the lobe. She heard his indrawn breath and smiled.

"I can think of a better place to celebrate your return," she murmured, her hand gliding down to where she could feel his need for her.

"You can?" he rasped, as her water-chilled fingers roamed over his warm skin.

"I can." She stepped out of his arms, and grinned. "If sir would like to follow me."

She retrieved a small plastic bag from under a broad, flat rock, and scooted up to the pull-in. Removing the key from the bag, she unlocked the car and opening the boot extracted a large towel.

Tucking it around her, she found a second one and folding it, placed it on the driver's seat. "This way, I don't have to get changed," she remarked — to Dominic's amusement — while she slipped her feet into a pair of sandals. "See you back at the cottage?" She raised a brow.

He nodded and walked around to his own vehicle at a smart clip. The drive to Salen seemed endless but was, in fact, less than twenty minutes, and soon they drew up at the rear of the house.

Dominic carried in Chloe's bags, while she dropped the two wet towels in the laundry sink.

"I'm going to take a shower," she said peeking around the door jamb into the kitchen."Fancy joining me?" Her innocent expression wasted when she gave him a wicked grin and ran her tongue over her top lip.

"Chloe, have you any idea what that does to a guy?"

"Not a clue. Would you like to show me?" She replied pertly and vanished up the stairs, Dominic hot on her heels.

Much, *much* later, they were enjoying a crisp turkey salad and a glass of white wine, talking about Chloe's upcoming interview.

Dominic had perused her portfolio and thought her selection captured just the right combination of themes.

"I was hoping to persuade you to live with me while you're working on this commission." Dominic ventured, while they washed the pots and tidied the kitchen.

Chloe mused over his proposal as she topped up their glasses. "You want that?" she asked curiously.

"Hell, yes!" His response instant and emphatic.

"Is it too soon?"

"What, us living together?"

She nodded

"Yep, totally too soon, but..."

As she blurted an interruption.

"... I don't care. I want you in my home, in my life, in my bed, every day, not just the odd weekend." He reached for her hand. "Chloe, I love you, more than my own life. Let's take a risk...?"

· · ·

Chloe searched his tawny gaze, the profound emotion in their hypnotic depths, made her heart sing. This was definitely *not* a cobweb dream.

"Let's..."

They sealed their decision with a passion that burned long into the night.

EPILOGUE
DECEMBER

A bitter wind whistled around the cottage. Flurries of sleet peppered the windows. It was three days before Christmas, and Chloe — hardly aware of the rising storm because of the music blaring from her iPod — was in a baking frenzy.

They had arrived three days ago, the car loaded down with more food than could possibly be consumed in a month never mind the two weeks they would be on Mull.

Dominic had meeting in Oban for meetings and was supposed to be back on the island today. The forecast was appalling, leaving Chloe to consider the possibility he might be delayed.

In the five months since her fateful holiday, much had happened. Her interview with the board of the Lanchester Hall Trust, lasted well over an hour.

Most of it was a relaxed conversation over coffee and cakes, discussing her ideas for the book and brochure — approval for the job, confirmed within the first ten minutes. The sum quoted as payment sounded astronomical to Chloe, but Alex assured her it was the going rate.

Chloe tried to talk them down because she wasn't a professional photographer, but Alex wouldn't hear of it.

"I've seen your photos. You have an eye for the unusual, for the shot taken from an angle no one would expect. I like that. It's exactly what we need. I'm also thinking we might pick one or two images to use on notepads and fridge magnets and so on.

"Now, and more importantly, are you completely recovered from your accident? Dominic told me," she elaborated at Chloe's puzzled frown. "I am very happy he found you. I was starting to think love would pass him by and he's such a great guy."

"I think so too," Chloe blushed, not used to her private life being under scrutiny.

Dominic, deep in discussion with Jake, Alex's husband, and some of the other board members, caught sight of Chloe's discomfiture. Excusing himself, he walked across the room to join the two women.

"Are you interrogating my Chloe?" he enquired of Alex who nodded.

"Of course! Your love life intrigues me." She beamed at him and then, giving him a hug, whispered in his ear "Don't let her go."

"I don't intend to," he replied, just as quietly.

"Right, my work here is done, time to get back to Rosedale. I look forward to working with you, Chloe."

That was the start of a whirlwind four months. Chloe went home for a few days to apprise Aunt Meg of her plans.

Her aunt remained a little sceptical that this new relationship was the *real thing*, but could not deny the change in Chloe. Her niece was glowing with happiness, so she kept her counsel content to observe from a distance.

Chloe took the opportunity to pop into her old place of work, where she said a proper goodbye, and then visited the old-folks home to explain her change in circumstances. Chloe's erstwhile colleagues and her elderly friends wished her every happiness.

Returning to Lanchester Hall, she settled herself and her few belongings into Dominic's apartment — a converted barn — which immediately felt as though she had lived there for ever. The following week was spent becoming acquainted with the estate, and its many facets.

By the time she set off for Mull, Chloe had accumulated well over a thousand images, covering summer, autumn, and the beginning of winter. Except for the Hall itself, the estate was quiet during the Christmas period, prompting Chloe to consider a fortnight's break and resume in January.

Dominic suggested Christmas on Mull, her comment about curling up in front of a roaring fire sipping whisky or hot chocolate, never far from his mind.

Chloe and Dominic were married at the end of October. Alex offered them the Hall for the ceremony and the reception, which bride and groom were pleased to accept — it was a generous gesture and, to be honest, the easiest option.

Aunt Meg and Chloe wrote to Chloe's parents, inviting them — without response. Chloe had long given up caring what her parents did or didn't do.

Dominic's family welcomed her with open arms. Gradually, she was becoming accustomed to being included in their lives.

Now, here she was, putting another batch of scones in the oven. Setting the timer for fifteen minutes, Chloe washed the huge pile of pots and tried to make the kitchen look less like a tornado had just blown through.

Going into the lounge, she put another log on the fire, and pottered about putting up the last few decorations. The timer pinged and Chloe checked the scones.

Surmising they were done, she left them to cool on a rack, and returned to the lounge with a cup of coffee.

Surveying the room, she smiled with satisfaction, it looked very cosy.

Her busy day caught up with her, and lulled by the flames leaping in the hearth, Chloe dozed off.

She was walking along the loch, it was a chilly day, a weak wintry sun was shining but the ground was blanketed in a hard frost, turning everything to silver.

The water was like smoky glass, a slight mist floating above it. Scrubby grass and spongy moss were strewn with silken cobwebs whose delicate, yet tenacious strands glistened like jewelled thread.

The sheer, breathtaking beauty of it resonated with Chloe. She reached for her camera, her artist's eye desperate to capture the moment. She didn't have it.

Out of nowhere, a stiff breeze whipped up, tugging at the cobwebs, tearing their gossamer filaments.

"Noooooooo!" She stretched her hand out to save them, but they were gone.

"Noooooo..." her cry echoed around the loch.

. . .

"Chloe... sweetheart, wake up,"

The voice was familiar. As was the hand touching her face, and the thumb tracing her bottom lip.

"Chloe."

She opened her eyes, her gaze colliding with that of her husband.

"Dominic?" She breathed his name, still trapped in the dream.

"Who else?" Mirth warming his question.

She came awake. He was here, in the cottage, sitting on the coffee table. "You made it. I thought you'd be delayed."

"Take more than bad weather to delay me, love. Okay, Mrs Winters, please tell me I smell cheese scones?"

She smiled, and he leaned across to kiss her lazily, sensuously.

"You do." She unfolded herself from the sofa and took his hand. "Come on, Mr Winters, time for Christmas to begin.

The weather turned icy, and by Christmas morning, Mull was dusted in a layer of fine snow.

After a leisurely breakfast, Chloe and Dominic drove, carefully, along Loch Na Keal, stopping at their favourite pull-in.

They were alone, no one else daring to venture out, which surprised Chloe — the dramatic scenery ought not to be missed. All was still, not a breath of air rippled the water — a storm-grey mirror reflecting the leaden sky.

The darkness that was Gribun soared in ominous majesty from the edge of the loch, disappearing into the clouds. The hoar frost covering the ground around them, glittered in myriad shades of white. Here and there, perfectly formed, wispy cobwebs clung to the peaty moss.

. . .

Chloe sucked in a breath.

"Oh, this has broken my dream," she murmured. "Look at the cobwebs. They remind me of our first week together. I was sure the whole thing was simply an illusion. One which would vanish like cobwebs in sunlight. Turns out, cobwebs are way more stubborn than I gave them credit for."

Dominic enfolded her in his arms and kissed her cold nose. "Your cobweb dream, hey?" Feeling her nod. He thought about that for a moment, then remarked, "Well, how about you be my cobweb…"

"Say what now…?" She pinned him with a quizzical glare.

"… let me finish, geez woman. You are my cobweb, but in reverse. I watch you spin your magic each morning. By evening you have created an exquisite whole, which I can spend the whole night unravelling. Something I get to do every day for the rest of my life."

Chloe nudged her husband, amused by his literary turn of phrase. "Dominic Winters, you do talk nonsense."

Tilting her head, she brushed her lips to his and smiled, a love immeasurable, glowing in her dove-grey eyes. "Although I do like the sound of that."

"See… and there's you thinking I don't have a sentimental bone in my body." He kissed her cold nose.

They strolled along the shore, chattering about this and that, their voices carrying in the quiet. Warm breath hanging like miniature clouds in the icy air. All too soon, snow began to drift down from the laden skies, spurring them to hurry back to the car — hot chocolate and other Christmas delicacies calling.

Chloe glanced over her shoulder when they drove away, wanting one last glimpse of that magical view. She sighed. Mull definitely knew how to weave her spell.

Hearing the soft sound, Dominic turned and smiled at her, his beautiful — yes, he was her husband she could call them beautiful — hazel eyes twinkling.

Chloe's heart swelled with unadulterated joy — she had all the magic she needed, right here.

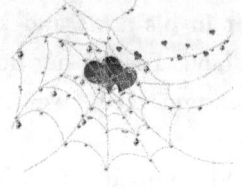

EXCERPT FROM HIS HEART'S SECOND SIGH

Reuben Faulkner stared at the papers spread out on the desk in front of him. All those years, and nothing, then... out of the blue... this. He couldn't decide how he felt but guessed he shouldn't be surprised. Leaning back in the chair he pinched the bridge of his nose, trying to release some of the tension. He would have to tell Jake. News of this magnitude could not be ignored or pushed under the table. Plus, he had a right to know — she was his mother after all.

Standing, Reuben walked over to gaze out of the window onto the stark beauty of the wintry garden with unseeing eyes. His vision was turned inward to the day before Erin left.

Thirty-four years earlier.

"Please Ben, just for once can we do something *I* want to do?" Erin's tone had taken on a grating, whiny quality, causing Reuben to frown.

"You know I can't get leave in the middle of semester, sweetheart. It's only a couple of months and we'll have the whole of the summer. We can go then. I can probably wangle six weeks."

"Yeah, you say that now, then there'll be a conference, or a dig or something you just *have* to attend or lead. Face it, Ben, you're more interested in lecturing and your PhD research than me."

Reuben gaped at the unfairness of his wife's accusation. "Erin, that's not true. We take holidays every year, none of which have remotely involved archaeology or conferences."

His thoughts winging to their last break, less than three months ago, when they'd visited her family and toured California.

"We just came back from a month in the States. I can't afford to go away every few weeks, love. You knew that when you married me. I am not some rich oil tycoon."

Erin pouted and, closing the gap to her husband, stretched up to brush a kiss to his lips, simultaneously walking her fingers up his shirt, fiddling with the buttons.

Reuben drew her against him to kiss her long and thoroughly, the ever-present desire flaring. At the same moment Erin began to undo his shirt, they were disturbed by a wail.

"Every time, it's like he knows... brat," Erin complained.

Reuben chuckled and disentangled himself. "Wait here, he probably just needs settling." He strolled along to the nursery, to spy their son standing at the rails of the cot, scrubbing his nose with his fist, his face flushed with temper.

"What's up, Jake?" Reuben lifted the child into his arms, taking the opportunity to rest the back of his hand on Jake's forehead. It felt a little warm but not overly so. "Did you have a bad dream?" he cooed, rhetorically, while rocking the child gently.

Jake snuggled into his father, nudging his head under Reuben's chin. In minutes he was fast asleep again. Reuben laid him carefully in the cot, and tucked a sheet around him, before covering half of his stocky little body with the blanket so he would not get hot.

He stood for moment studying his son. The familiar yet inexplicable joy, he was somehow partly responsible for producing such a perfect child, washed over him and, unable to help himself, he ran a tender finger along Jake's cheek.

"He always responds better to you." Erin's voice drifted to him from the doorway. He turned to see his wife leaning on the door jamb, her lovely features marred by discontent. Reuben swallowed a sigh.

"Pure imagination, darling. He loves us both the same, it's just he sees me more because I drop him at the Uni childcare centre."

Erin, who hadn't worked a day since their marriage and had no other call on her time, refused to be a stay-at-home mother. She declared she had no intention of being tied to a kitchen sink or a squalling child. That's what day-care was for.

Thankfully, Reuben's job entitled him to make use of the childcare facility on campus and, although he hated leaving Jake there while he was lecturing, at least the child was well looked after.

He felt the frown returning. Erin had changed so much. Gone was the carefree spirit he fell in love with. She was always irritated either with him or Jake, and he couldn't remember the last time she had done anything spontaneous, not even a smile. He didn't know what was wrong. When he asked, she shrugged and said she was fine.

He knew she chafed at the quiet of Moorview, their home in the village of Rosedale Abbey. She had begged him to move several times, but he could not bear to sell up. The Yorkshire moors were his solace and, especially after a busy term, his haven. They had talked about buying a flat in Durham, so Erin was closer to Newcastle and all it had to offer, but so far it had not come to fruition. Everything they looked at was too small.

Erin was from San Francisco. Her family's home was huge, two stories, with a tennis court and a pool. Compared with North Yorkshire, where the weather had a tendency to be unpredictable, San Francisco always seemed warm and sunny — quite attractive, he supposed, if you liked that sort of thing.

Reuben much preferred the four definite seasons. In actual fact, when he really thought about it, Erin and he were vastly different in outlook. That was probably what drew them together, they were the epitome of opposites attract.

They fell in love, at least Reuben had, but lately, he was not so sure about Erin. They married very young, and for the last four years he thought they were happy. He certainly was. As he scanned Erin's face, he realised she was miserable, and his heart cracked a little.

With a final glance at Jake to make sure he was asleep, Reuben walked over to his wife and took her in his arms.

"I'm sorry, love. I know you struggle being here all day. How about we go check out some apartments this weekend?"

He deliberately used the term Erin was more accustomed to, because it made them sound considerably larger than they actually were.

"Might be worth going down to York and seeing what they have available. It'd be just as easy for me to get to work from there as here."

He kissed her nose, her cheek, then scattered light kisses along her throat. He heard her sigh as she angled her head exposing the soft skin of her neck, and felt her fingers worming under his shirt.

Lifting Erin, Reuben carried her along to their bedroom and spent the next little while demonstrating just how much he loved her.

When he woke the next morning, she was gone.

At first, Reuben tried to persuade himself Erin had just decided to take an early morning stroll, or perhaps a drive. Hours ticked by and, with no evidence she was returning any time soon, he conceded his wife's disappearance was far more serious.

Even now, over three decades later, he recalled his sense of absolute shock and fury that she had walked away, after their night of passionate lovemaking.

Then the questions began hammering into his mind. Why had she gone? Was there someone else? How had she managed to leave without him hearing her? What about Jake? Their beautiful son had slept through his father's panic, supremely oblivious to the confusion.

Reuben had rung his widowed mother, who dropped everything to come and stay. Sarah Faulkner never trusted Erin, whom she believed had anticipated being the wife of an academic would be glamorous. Lecture tours to exotic places, wining and dining in the hallowed halls of prestigious universities, black-tie balls, long holidays to faraway lands.

Instead of which she found herself married to a hard-working, rather reserved lecturer, who enjoyed a peaceful existence on the edge of the moors and who, other than participating in the occasional archaeological dig, seldom left England.

Children had not been part of Erin's plan either. She wanted to be free to come and go as she pleased, not be restricted by a pesky, needy, clingy rugrat... her words.

From the moment Jake was born, Reuben had done everything for their son. Even in the hospital, Erin showed little interest in the child she had brought into the world. She rarely held Jake, and Reuben could not recall her ever cuddling him, or rocking him to sleep when he was teething or unwell.

Now, just when Jake was about to turn three, his mother had upped and vanished.

When he looked back, Reuben could not fathom how he muddled through those first few days, which fast became weeks. He informed the police of Erin's disappearance and, after waiting the obligatory forty-eight hours — Erin was an adult and entitled to do as she pleased — they instigated a search.

Her car was found at York train station and it was quickly established she had travelled to Kings Cross and onto Heathrow, where she had boarded a flight to San Francisco via New York. There the trail ended.

Reuben rang her family, sent letters, and telegrams. It was as though she had never existed, no one would tell him anything. Eventually, her grandmother bowed under his constant calls, and confirmed Erin was safe and well, but she wanted nothing to do with him.

There was no accusation of ill-treatment, no claim he had not been a doting husband, Erin simply did not want to be married to him anymore.

Initially, Reuben had sent updates about Jake, but they petered out when he received no response. Neither did he hear from a lawyer with regards to Erin wanting a divorce. After a few years, she faded into the background. He did not forget her, he had loved her too much, but it was easier to cope if he consigned her to his past.

———

Now she was suddenly very much a part of his present.

ABOUT THE AUTHOR

Rosie Chapel lives in Perth, Australia with her hubby and three furkids. When not writing, she loves catching up with friends, burying herself in a book (or three), discovering the wonders of Western Australia, or — and the best — a quiet evening at home with her husband, enjoying a glass of wine and a movie.

Website: www.rosiechapel.com

OTHER BOOKS BY ROSIE CHAPEL

Fate is Curious

A Christmas Prayer with Ashlee Shades

The Lady's Wager

Winning Emma

A Love Impossible

Unravelling Roana

Fairy Tale Romance

Chasing Bluebells

Contemporary Romances

Of Ruins and Romance

All At Once It's You

Cobweb Dreams

Just One Step

His Heart's Second Sigh

HISTORICAL FICTION

The Pomegranate Tree

Hannah's Heirloom - Book One

Hoping to trace the origins of an ancient ruby clasp, a gift from her long dead grandmother, Hannah Wilson travels to the fortress of Masada with her best friend, Max. Strange dreams concerning a rebel ambush begin to haunt Hannah and following a tragic accident, she slips into the world of Ancient Masada.

A woman out of time, Hannah must rely on her instincts and her knowledge of what will befall this citadel to survive. Will she escape, or is she doomed to die along with hundreds of others as Masada falls – and what does any of this have to do with an ancient ruby clasp?

Echoes of Stone and Fire

Hannah's Heirloom - Book Two

Pompeii - a vibrant city lost in time following the AD79 eruption of Vesuvius. Now rediscovered, archaeologists yearn for an opportunity to uncover the town's past. Some things, however, are best left alone - revealing the secrets hidden beneath the stones could prove perilous. Hannah and Max are brought to Pompeii by a surprise invitation to join an excavation team who are trying to uncover the city's long history.

After entering an excavated house that bears a Hebrew inscription, Hannah's two worlds collide, and she falls back through time to ancient Pompeii. A place where her ancestor is a physician to gladiators engaged in mortal combat, where riotous mobs run amok and where a ghost from the past returns to haunt her.

Will Hannah and her loved ones manage to escape the devastation she knows is coming, before the town is engulfed in volcanic ash? Will she ever find her way back to Max the love of her life, waiting not so patiently millennia away? Or will echoes be all that remain?

Embers of Destiny

Hannah's Heirloom - Book Three

AD80 - Hannah and Maxentius must embark on a new journey to Northern Britannia. This harsh frontier is far from the comforts of Rome and danger lurks where least expected; a garrison of soldiers, some unhappy with their isolated posting; local tribes, outwardly accepting of their Roman occupier, but who may still resent the seizure of their lands.

Millennia away, Hannah Vallier finds a familiar item while working in a museum near Hadrian's Wall. It is the pomegranate; carved by Maxentius on Masada. Before Hannah can discuss it with Max, disaster strikes! Believing her husband has been killed, Hannah retreats into the past, her soul melding with that of her ancestor, but with little idea of what they could face. Is the risk from the conquered tribes, or much closer to home?

As rebellion threatens to shatter a fragile peace, Hannah's heart whispers that just maybe Max isn't dead and that he is calling her home. Can she trust her heart, or will she remain caught out of time, her destiny floating away like embers on a breeze?

Etched in Starlight

Hannah's Heirloom - Prequel

Maxentius - a Roman soldier fresh from the battlefields of Armenia, arrives to take command of the military outpost of Masada, Herod's isolated citadel in the Judaean desert. A seemingly mundane posting after years of warfare, Maxentius finds it more challenging to maintain a focused garrison than to face the wrath of the Parthians across a disputed frontier.

Hannah - a young Hebrew physician spends her days dealing with injuries from street brawls, deprivation, disease and loss. As her beloved Jerusalem plunges into chaos; her brother — who belongs to a band of rebels determined to drive out their Roman occupiers — tells her of their plans to storm a desert fortress and steal the weapons stored there, persuading his reluctant sister to go with him.

Masada - following the ambush, Hannah finds and treats three badly wounded Roman soldiers. In the aftermath and against impossible odds, Hannah and Maxentius realise that they are more than healer and captive, their fate already etched in starlight.

Prelude to Fate

For Lucia, staring into the jaws of an horrific death, escape seems impossible.

Rufius Atellus, a veteran Roman soldier, is appalled when he recognises one of the victims about to be executed. Surely this is a ghastly mistake?

A ferocious she-wolf, anticipating a tasty meal, suddenly finds herself under a human's control.

In an unexpected twist, and as danger threatens, the lives of all three become inextricably entwined.

Was it chance brought them together in that theatre of bloodshed, or simply a prelude to fate?

REGENCY ROMANCE

Once Upon An Earl

Linen and Lace - Book One

When Fate saw fit to intervene in the life of Giles Trevallier, the very respectable Earl of Winchester, by dropping a female — soaked to the skin and with no memory of who she is or how she came to be there — literally at his feet, no one could have predicted the outcome.

While uncovering her identity, Giles realises he is falling hopelessly in love with his mystery guest, who unbeknownst to him, is succumbing to similar emotions; but, when the heart is involved, a thoughtless word or gesture can thwart even Fate's best-laid plans.

Faced with misunderstandings, whispers of scandal, secret documents and foreign agents, their chance at a happy ever after seems elusive, but fairy tales often happen when least expected, and love — however inconvenient — usually finds a way to conquer all.

To Unlock Her Heart

Linen and Lace - Book Two

Abused by a duke, and shunned by Society, relief seems at hand when Grace Aldeburgh is bequeathed a house in a small village, far from malicious gossips.

Once there, a tentative friendship blooms between Grace and Theo Elliott, the local doctor, who has already resolved to be the man to unlock her heart.

Just when happiness appears to be within her grasp, her erstwhile tormentor once again stalks Grace. After a failed kidnap attempt, the duke's quest culminates in an acrimonious confrontation, and the reason for his venal pursuit becomes agonisingly clear.

Love on a Winter's Tide

Linen and Lace - Book Three

Every day, Helena disappears into a world few acknowledge, helping the poor, downtrodden, and abused. A husband is the last thing she can be bothered with.

Busy managing his shipping line, Hugh Drummond sees no need for a wife, whose only joy is dancing and frivolity. If — and it was a huge if — he ever married, it would be to a woman as capable as he, not some giddy society Miss.

Then, Hugh meets Helena and despite their resolve, fate, it seems, has other ideas. As their attraction deepens however, treachery threatens to tear them apart. Will they uncover the perpetrator in time, or will their love be swept away, lost forever on a winter's tide?

A Love Unquenchable

Linen and Lace - Book Four

Jessica Drummond, a bright and cheerful young woman, rarely gives romance, let alone love, a thought. Long hours working in her brother's shipping office affords little chance of her ever meeting an eligible bachelor.

Duncan Barrington, veteran of the Napoleonic Wars, believes himself wounded in both body and soul. He has no intention of inflicting his demons on anyone, certainly not a beautiful and, in his opinion, irresponsible city lady.

One cold and snowy morning, the plight of a bedraggled puppy throws Jessica and Duncan together and, as a spark of something indefinable yet wholly unquenchable begins to burn, it is unclear who rescued whom.

A Hidden Rose

Linen and Lace - Book Five

After witnessing his mother's grief at the loss of his father, Nick Drummond resolved never to cause someone he loved such distress. Even the happiness of his siblings would not sway him – until he met Rose.

Rose Archer was almost content assisting her doctor father in a tiny fishing village in the north of Yorkshire. To experience the world beyond, a tantalising dream – until she met Nick.

Unexpectedly, the impossible becomes possible, and the renounced – desired above all things, but the shipwreck that brought them together, may yet tear them apart. Will Nick learn to trust his heart, or will his love for Rose remain forever hidden

---

The Daffodil Garden

A Regency Romance

Horrifically scarred during the war, William Harcourt - Marquis of Blackthorne - prefers to spend his days in the quiet of his daffodil garden; plants do not pity, turn away, or judge.

Lucy Truscott, whose life is far removed from that of the *ton*, has no idea that by saving the life of a young woman, to whom she bears an uncanny resemblance, her own will be placed in mortal danger.

A chance encounter leads to something more. William begins to trust that Lucy sees the man beneath the scars, while Lucy is persuaded that love might actually transcend status.

Unfortunately, before their courtship has really begun, someone has every intention of ending it - permanently.

The Unconventional Duchess

A Regency Romance

Refusing to suffer the humiliation of her husband flaunting his mistress at Society events, the newly married Duchess of Wallingstead, Ella Lennox, takes control of her life. She leaves London for the family's country seat in remote Yorkshire.

A woman alone, Ella spends the next four years turning a cold, grim house into a home, and transforming the fortunes of the estate. Not afraid of hard work, she soon earns the respect of those around her with her determination and unconventional attitude.

Out of the blue, the duke arrives. Resigned to another arduous visit, Ella is stunned when it seems he is attempting to court her.

Impossible!

Could her dream of a happy marriage be about to come true?

Everything hangs on a snowstorm, a herd of cows and an uninvited guest!

Rescuing Her Knight

The de Wiltons - Book One

A story, invented to keep a little girl distracted, marks the beginning of another tale. One destined to remain unfinished for nearly twenty years.

Against her better judgement, Kitty de Wilton is persuaded to help Adam Marchmain banish his demons. This requires a subterfuge which, if discovered, might shatter more than the bonds of friendship forged two decades previously.

To Kitty, determined to break through the shield Adam has erected, the risk is worth it.

To see his smile and hear his laughter.

To rescue the knight of her childhood.

Just when a fairy tale ending is within her grasp, Kitty is threatened by the man who murdered her husband. In a cruel twist the tables are turned, and Kitty is the one who needs rescuing.

His Fiery Hoyden

A Regency Novella

Livvy has no respect for the nobility; they let her down when she most needed them. Why should she accede to their demands now?

Philip, Lord Harrington, is stunned to discover the young heir to the dukedom lives a stone's throw away in a ramshackle cottage, and resolves to restore the child to his birthright.

They meet in a clash of wills, but just when it seems Livvy might surrender, the victory Philip desires, may not taste all that sweet.

A Regency Duet

Luck be a Pirate

Luck wasn't something retired pirate Kennet Alexson believed in – good or bad. However, even he had to concede that landing a job at Trentams shipyard, and meeting Lynette Collins, was more than coincidence.

Fortune it seemed, was smiling on him for once.

As Kennet adjusts to life on dry land, his friendship with Lynette deepens into something far more enduring, and what once seemed elusive now becomes possible.

Unfortunately, fate has other plans, and Kennet's good luck is about to run out.

The Highwayman's Kiss

Nothing exciting had ever happened to Juliette St Clair. Her days were spent assisting her father or calling on friends, wandering art galleries, taking constitutionals or, and more preferably, escaping into her books. Her evenings her evenings — an endless round of balls, where she preferred to remain invisible.

Until the day she was robbed by a highwayman.

A Regency Christmas Double

Heart Rescued

Four years since Jasper lost the woman he was hoping to marry. Four years since he closed his heart and withdrew from Society. He has no idea his reclusive existence is about to be shattered.

Enter his sister's best friend, Harriet, a flame haired beauty, who needs his help.

Reluctantly he agrees and as they spend time together, it is clear their feelings run deep. Although Harriet affects Jasper in a way no woman ever has, he believes her to be out of his league ~ but it's Christmas and she might just be the one to melt his frozen heart

Catch a Snowflake

Romance often blossoms in the most unlikely of places - but in a ward full of wounded soldiers - surely not?

When Lucas Withers comes face to face with Jemima Parsons - a young woman who blames him for her brother's injury - falling in love is the last thing on their minds. What neither of them anticipated, was the magic of snowflakes.

Fate is Curious

A Regency Novella

Happily, ever after? No such thing! Bereft, following her beloved husband's sudden death, Lady Charlotte Sherbrooke has lost her belief in such romantic nonsense.

Successful shipping merchant, Zacharie Romain, is no stranger to loss; his business can be hazardous. Moreover, his wife died in childbirth and even though it happened a decade ago, he has no mind to expose himself to such sorrow again.

They meet in less than joyful circumstances but, as the year turns and grief diminishes, the woes of a small boy become the catalyst for something wholly unexpected. Can Charlotte and Zacharie trust what Fate has in store or will past heartbreak prevent them from taking a chance on love?

A Christmas Prayer

with Ashlee Shades

A Short Story

An entreaty from a frightened child.

Orphaned and only nine, Caroline Thorne has to grow up before her time. She is doing everything she can to keep what is left of her family together and out of the workhouse but is terrified her prayers are not being heard. Or maybe they are...

A petition from a woman desperate for a family.

A chance meeting with three orphaned siblings, tugs at Elizabeth Barrington's heart strings. Thus far, she and her husband have not been blessed with children and, as Christmas approaches, a plan begins to form - one which might just be the answer to her prayers.

Two Christmas prayers, as different as they are the same.

Will they hear and, more importantly, heed the answer?

The Lady's Wager

Surrendered Hearts- Book Two

A Novelette

Ged Mowbray will do anything to avoid being married off to the suitable prospects his parents insist on parading in front of him.

Melissa Bouchard is under no illusion her sizeable dowry is the attraction to suitors, not her.

An overheard conversation leads to an offer too good to refuse, but what happens when a lady's wager, becomes a gamble on the happily ever after, you did not even realise you wanted?

Winning Emma

Surrendered Hearts - Book Three

A Novelette

Randolph Craythorpe — earl, covert operative, and occasional highwayman — believed his dalliance with Lady Felicity Hartwich would lead to marriage. It did, but not to him! The arrival of an unwelcome guest, however, provides the perfect opportunity to indulge in a little retaliation.

Emma Newbury accompanies her cousin, Lady Charity Anscombe, to London for the Christmas season. Once there, she comes face to face with the three men who witnessed the humiliating aftermath of her father's disgrace — one of whom, to her irritation, has taken up residence in her dreams.

Their infrequent encounters only serve to confuse but, while winter tightens its grip on the city, what was inconceivable becomes the one thing for which they both yearn, yet bound by Society's rules, cannot admit.

As the snow falls, Randolph begins to understand that to win Emma, he will have to surrender.

A Love Impossible

A Regency M/M Novelette

Tasked with investigating a heinous crime, Edward Lindsay travels from London to Dublin — a city which holds too many memories — in the guise of guardian to his sister. He knew it could be hazardous, and relished the challenge, but that wasn't what caused his stomach to tighten as they approached landfall.

Dublin held more than just a murderer.

There was also Aidan.

While attending a party, Aidan Griffen is astonished when he comes face to face with a man who fled Dublin two years previously. A man he has desperately tried to forget.

As Edward closes in on his quarry, a fire, deliberately extinguished, is rekindled. But what of it? Edward and Aidan share a love impossible, and to acknowledge their feelings — more dangerous than confronting a killer.

Is there any hope of a happily ever after?

Unravelling Roana

Tired of being ignored by her husband, Roana Dumont, Countess of Brooketon does the one thing guaranteed to get his attention. She runs away... to Venice, leaving behind a set of riddles for him to solve... *if* he feels their marriage is worth saving.

Gideon Dumont, 6th Earl of Brooketon is flabbergasted when he discovers his wife has apparently vanished off the face of the earth. A series of puzzles, the only clue as to her whereabouts.

The question is... will he unravel them?

FAIRY TALE ROMANCE

Chasing Bluebells

A Novella

Once upon a time, somewhere in France, there was a man whose reckless obsession led him down a dark path — one which, ultimately, cost him his life. That ought to have been the end of it. Regrettably, as is so often the case, those who least deserve it, suffer for the actions of others.

A decade after being sent away, Sebastien Daviau returns to the little village where everything began. Hoping to lay the ghosts of his childhood to rest, he studiously ignores the possibility, he might run into Charlotte de Montbeliard.

As luck would have it, Charlotte is the one who runs into him... well, his horse... and although the brief encounter leaves a lasting impression, neither recognises the other.

A name revealed causes a freak accident, catapulting Sebastien's past into his present, and bringing him face to face with a man whose reputation would intimidate the most ardent of suitors.

Can whatever is blossoming between Charlotte and Sebastien survive the challenge imposed, or is their happily ever after about to fade as quickly as the bluebells they loved to chase?

CONTEMPORARY ROMANCES

Of Ruins and Romance

While escorting a group of tourists around the ancient Roman port of Ostia, Kassandra Winters bumps into someone she first met in less than auspicious circumstances two years previously. The encounter leads to a job offer - to be the assistant guide for a three-week tour of ancient sites in and around Rome. Unable to resist such an opportunity, Kassie agrees.

Kassie has intrigued Gabriel St Germain since he accidentally knocked her flying outside her university professor's office. Her face haunts his dreams, yet he never expected to see her again. So, he is surprised when she appears, as though destined to do so, in the middle of a ruin, and he concocts a plan to win her heart.

Gabriel's old-fashioned courtship touches something deep inside Kassie and, although struggling to believe someone as handsome as Gabriel could possibly be interested in her, she soon realises she has fallen irrevocably in love with him. However, just as Kassie shares everything of herself with Gabriel, her world comes crashing down. Can their romance survive, or will it fall in ruins, like the relics of antiquity that brought them together?

All At Once It's You

When Alex arrives in the small village of Rosedale Abbey, to take up a position as a research assistant for a renowned archaeologist, the last thing she is looking for, or expects to find, is love.

Jake was perfectly happy with the status quo. When it came to relationships, he didn't do committed or long term. He called the shots, and if his current flame didn't like it, she knew what to do. A philosophy, which served him well - until he met Alex.

Romance blooms, but even as the untamed wilderness of the North Yorkshire moors weaves its spell, a long-buried secret might yet jeopardise their happily ever after.

Just One Step

A Short Story

In the aftermath of an horrific car accident, Daisy Forrester travels to Italy - hoping, so far from her memories, she might begin to heal.

Archaeologist, and single father, Adam Willoughby is too busy looking after his young daughter to give romance let alone love, a thought.

Neither expects a chance encounter in an ancient ruin to be anything more, but sometimes, that's all it takes.

His Heart's Second Sigh

A Novella

Reuben Faulkner and Paige Latimer are two happily single people, who have no desire to upset the status quo.

Unexpectedly, they are thrown together, only to discover both want far more than a casual friendship.

Just when things take an interesting turn, Reuben's past catches up with them, and threatens to derail their blossoming romance before it has chance to start.

www.ingramcontent.com/pod-product-compliance
Lightning Source LLC
Chambersburg PA
CBHW070614120726
47909CB00004B/1213